WINTER'S MAZE

WINTER BLACK SERIES: SEASON TWO BOOK EIGHT

MARY STONE

MARY
STONE
PUBLISHING

Copyright © 2024 by Mary Stone Publishing

All rights reserved.

No part of this book may be reproduced in any form or by any electronic or mechanical means, including information storage and retrieval systems, without written permission from the author, except for the use of brief quotations in a book review.

❀ Created with Vellum

For Aunt Ann,

Tiny in stature but mighty in spirit. Though life bent your body, it never dimmed your light. I miss you. RIP.

DESCRIPTION

Achievement unlocked. One wrong move, and it's game over.

Private detective Winter Black finally knows the identity of the puppeteer behind the recent string of murders she's been entangled in investigating—the same man who's been stalking and tormenting her for weeks. But when he leaves recent photographs he took of her and Noah, her husband's eyes scratched out, his vendetta becomes frighteningly real. And terrifyingly personal.

Because Noah is missing.

The nightmare becomes disturbingly real when Noah's wedding band is placed on Winter's doorstep, accompanied by a taunting note written in cryptic, video game jargon. The instructions? A deadly scavenger hunt, with Noah's life hanging in the balance. Refusing to play isn't an option.

Her mission: find her husband before it's too late.

As Winter dives headfirst into the puppeteer's sinister game, other unwilling players emerge, their fates as uncertain as Noah's. Every clue leads her deeper into a labyrinth of danger, each wrong move tightening the noose around the man she loves. The stakes couldn't be higher: solve the puzzle or lose Noah forever.

The mystery and suspense continue with Winter's Maze, the eighth book in the Winter Black Season Two series. The game is far from over. In fact, it's only just begun.

1

Three months earlier...

Willa York jabbed the power button on the screwed-down remote, silencing the TV. Even as the room quieted, the musky motel air seemed to grow thicker and louder, an unwelcome reminder of just how far she'd fallen.

She sank back against the lumpy mattress, cursing as the springs poked into her ribs. Every distraction she'd tried had failed.

Half a pint of whiskey—no help.

A crying jag that left her eyes raw—useless.

Even *The Notebook* hadn't done the trick. If Ryan Gosling's soulful eyes couldn't drag her out of this pit, what could?

She contemplated the threadbare carpet, the flickering streetlight casting jittery shadows as restless as ghosts. Like a moth drawn to a flame, her gaze turned to her phone on the nightstand, the screen's glow cutting through the dimness. Maybe Rich—both the love and loss of her life—had called. Or texted.

Or maybe he was dead in a ditch somewhere. Honestly, that might've been easier to deal with.

No messages. The time read 2:34 a.m. She tossed the phone onto the bed.

Just last week, they'd rung in the New Year. They were happy, or so she thought.

Sighing so hard her lungs ached, Willa hugged one of the flat pillows to her chest. None of her usual breakup rituals worked this time. And going to that bar with Chelsea? Big mistake. Chelsea's loose lips had let the truth tumble out—Rich had been cheating for months.

That bitch. Some best friend she was, keeping their dirty little secret so long.

After everything she'd sacrificed and suffered for the man she considered her soulmate, Willa had never felt more used, more betrayed.

She could still see his stupid gerbil face looking up at her all confused. Like he was going to try to play it off. She'd caught him with his pants down, literally, and he still had the nerve to look her in the eye and say, *"It's not what you think."* He squealed all wide-eyed as he wiggled himself from underneath Missy, straddling him on their couch.

Her couch!

She was the one who bought that couch with the money from her receptionist job when she, Chelsea, and Missy decided to get an apartment together. And Missy just sat up with a shrug. No apology, no nothing. She'd almost looked happy, the sinister bitch.

"I could kill the bastard!" Hopping up from the bed in a fit of rage, Willa grabbed her duffel and dumped its contents all over the floor. Her underwear, unpaired socks, blouse, and jeans were wrinkled as shit, her load of laundry sitting in the dryer, still damp, when everything in her life shattered into pieces.

What the hell is this?

She held up a slinky rayon thing. It was the sinister bitch's favorite dress.

Willa should've been happy she'd inadvertently taken side-chick special, but just a glimpse of the skanky sequins created a wave of agony that threatened to drown her. A wail clawed its way from her throat, and she broke into fresh tears.

Stumbling into the bathroom, Willa fell to her knees beside the tub. She cranked on the faucet and shoved her head under the freezing water, drenching her hair and the back of her neck. As the water tickled her nose and snaked into her mouth, she let out a scream and kept it up until her voice hurt, until her lungs ached, until she had nothing left.

The water warmed as her screams faded. She didn't want to cry anymore. The bastard didn't deserve any of her tears. But she couldn't stop herself. Her stomach lurched, and she dry-heaved into the tub.

With shaky fingers, Willa turned off the water. Her shoulders shook, her chest heaved. She shouldn't have drunk so much whiskey. Everything in the room was swimming—especially the tiny blue floor tiles. They looked like little fish in a dizzy stream.

The water from her wet head dampened the neck of her *Vote for Pedro* t-shirt, dripping down onto her loose jeans with the huge holes in the knees. She snatched a towel from the bar and wrapped her hair into a turban.

For a long time, she sat by the tub like that, the same thought circling through her head again and again.

I could break him. One phone call, and I could break him.

He was the one who should've been crying in a puddle of his own filth, not her. In fact, he should've been in prison. Everything she'd suffered, she had for his sake, to keep him from a worse fate. She saved him that day when she copped to driving the car that accidentally killed a pedestrian. He was off his rocker, again. Drunk. High. He had offenses.

If she'd let him take the fall, he would have been put away for years, and she'd loved him too much to let that happen. He was going to be her husband someday. She'd taken the fall in a vehicular homicide for the would-be father of her fucking children, only to find him grinding on her roommate.

Now he was nothing.

This is over, Rich.

The son of a bitch would finally get his due.

"Where's my phone?" Willa stumbled to her feet. She reached out to catch herself and accidentally yanked one end of the towel bar away from the wall.

Lurching out of the bathroom, she fell on the queen bed at the center of the room. It was still neatly made, since she hadn't had the energy to change or crawl under the covers.

Grabbing her phone from where it rested on the duvet, she pulled up the number for the Austin Police Department. A cool breeze brushed over her cheek, and she shivered. Looking up, she realized the hotel door hung open an inch.

A sobering shot of fear seized her heart. She hopped up from the bed and scurried to the door. Throwing it open, she peered out into the night.

The parking lot lay silent but for the whoosh of the distant freeway and the dull trundle of a train.

Maybe she'd left it open? She was pretty drunk, after all.

With a light laugh to ease her nerves, Willa shut the door firmly. As she returned to the bed, she looked down at her phone. At the number. Could she really do this?

Her finger hovered over the Call button.

Just do—

Something slammed into the back of her head, propelling her into the TV stand. Too surprised to even cry out, she bounced off and hit the floor. Blood pooled in her mouth, swimming between her teeth, causing her to gag when she tried to scream.

Her body sagged, her vision blurred, and her head pulsed with pain.

Had she passed out? Had the combination of alcohol and tears been too much?

Turning over, she gasped as a shadow moved above her. The figure was distorted, as though she were peering through warped glass. The edges of his form wavered, details smearing together into a featureless blur. As he bent closer, the scene sharpened, and details clicked into place like a sinister puzzle.

Dark hood pulled low over his face. Surgical mask covering his mouth and nose. Clear goggles ringing his eyes. White hazmat jumpsuit.

"It shouldn't have come to this."

As though her limbs knew what to do without being told, she scurried back but could only move a few inches before she cracked her head into the wall. She scrambled up to her feet. "Take my money! Take anything you want. Please!"

"Do I look like I came here for money?" He slammed his hands onto the wall on either side of her, trapping her.

Willa ducked beneath his arm, but he snatched her by the waist and held her in place as she kicked out at him.

"Help me! Somebody!" Swinging her arms wildly, she connected a fist with his face. He doubled over, giving her a split second to struggle free. Panting, she darted for the door.

The man grabbed her ankle, pulling her feet out from under her.

Her nose met the floor before the rest of her body. Blood burst over her already bloody lips.

The man rolled her over and straddled her. Bucking beneath him, she flailed her arms, trying to catch him with her nails. He caught her wrists and pinned her arms under his knees. Before Willa could think what to do next, his hands wrapped around her throat.

Willa thrashed her legs, trying to kick free, but he was so strong and heavy. His body weight crushed her lungs while his fingers squeezed her windpipe. She twisted back and forth. Her arms finally broke free, and she scratched at his hands, but her thick, blunt acrylics did no damage. She felt around for something, anything, that could serve as a weapon. Her blow-dryer was within reach, by all the crap from her open duffel bag.

She wrapped her fingers around the handle and smacked him as hard as she could. It bounced off his shoulder.

"Don't fight." His grip eased off just a little.

She sucked in a gasp of breath.

"The least you could do is accept your punishment. You know you deserve this. You have to."

"I didn't...I can't."

The glittering light from the window flashed on his goggles, and Willa caught the barest glimpse of watery brown eyes hiding behind them, wild with animalistic anger.

"You know what you did, Willa York." He squeezed her throat tighter than before, shaking her like a rag doll. "You thought you'd get away with it too. Not on my watch. Not on my fucking watch! Do you hear me?"

What had she done? The car accident? Stepping in for Rich? Was that what her assailant meant? It was always on her mind, but it was also so long ago...and no one knew about it.

Shaking her by the throat, he smacked the back of her head against the carpet again and again, the dull thuds echoing in her skull like the pounding of distant drums. Pain shot through her in jagged waves, her vision tilting and spinning as she fought for the smallest breath. She clawed at his arms, but her strength melted with every blow, her muscles unresponsive, her body betraying her.

Just like everyone does.

As darkness crept in at the edges of her vision, his voice became her world, each vicious word blurring into a guttural roar of rage. The world around her fractured—sounds too sharp, the carpet fibers biting into her scalp like needles. Her chest heaved, desperate for air that refused to come.

As though a switch had been flipped, the pain faded, and her body sank into a terrible stillness. Her mind followed as sight and sound mercifully eased.

It was over.

2

Present time...

Road construction around her office left Winter Black-Dalton twitching behind the wheel. Of all the days. She had to get home to Noah. It was eleven thirty-five on a Tuesday morning, five whole minutes since she'd found the terrible photo of her beloved husband's eyes and mouth scratched out.

Answer the phone, dammit.

As it rang, she cursed the fact that it was spring, the time of year when the city normally worked on the roads. Couldn't they see how desperate she was to get home to her husband—to hold him in her arms and see for herself that he was okay? Until then, there was no way to slow her heartbeat, no way to keep her teeth from grinding.

The photographs she'd found on her windshield lay in a disorganized pile on her passenger seat. Half a dozen showed her and Noah together—out on their first date in what seemed like years—not knowing the entire time they were being stalked by a murderer.

Erik Saulson was his name. Or that was what his former associate had called him before he murdered her in the back alley of her apartment.

Cybil Kerie had worked for psychologist Dr. Ava Poole. But her true reason for employment at the Blue Tree Wellness Center had been to frame Dr. Poole for murder—murders Cybil committed to exact revenge on the psychologist for breaking up her parents' marriage, which led to her mother's death by suicide when Cybil was just thirteen.

When Winter and Noah confronted Cybil at her apartment, they learned Erik Saulson was the real puppeteer behind the scheme to hypnotize Dr. Poole's patients into taking their own lives. Cybil said Erik was evil and hated Winter. Why, the young woman did not know.

But Noah couldn't find any history on the man, and Noah was no slouch when it came to research.

The voice message Saulson had sent Winter just minutes ago had self-deleted, like all the others. Winter had been playing against him long enough to anticipate that, and she'd uploaded it to the cloud before even opening the message.

Winter slammed on the brakes, stuck on a one-lane road behind a dump truck and an excavator. She was trapped. If she thought it'd be any faster to get out of the SUV and run, she would've done just that. She called Noah again. No answer. She called her grandparents and asked Gramma Beth if she'd seen him.

"Not since the last time the two of you came over. Are you all right, dearie?"

"I'm fine. I'll call you later. Love you." Disconnecting the call, Winter punched her fist against the dash as the dump truck lurched two feet forward. She snatched the steering wheel with both hands and swung her body back and forth, wishing she had a police siren in her vehicle. Not that it would've been any help right now. It'd take more than a siren to get out of this. More like the damn Batmobile.

Winter opened Saulson's voice message and played it a second time.

"Well played, Winter."

His tenor voice had little depth, as if he were speaking only with the front of his mouth. She could hear the saliva pooling under his tongue as he taunted her. She'd followed his stupid clues, played his game, and found the identity of his accomplice.

"You cheesed your way right through Cybil's silly little game like I knew you would."

Cheesed her way through? What the hell did that mean? The only time she'd heard *cheesed* used as a verb was when Shaggy told Scooby-Doo to cheese it so they could run away from the carnival owner dressed as a ghost.

Was that what he meant? She ran through his game?

"She was just bullet fodder anyway. That's right, I killed her."

He sounded so proud—like a child telling his mom he got an A on an art project.

Winter paused the voicemail as a construction worker in a neon vest twirled his sign from *STOP* to *SLOW*. She eased her foot off the brake and followed the dump truck between orange cones at a snail's pace to the other side of the one-way stretch.

No traffic jam had ever infuriated her more.

When they finally reached the end of the construction, the road opened up. She stomped down hard on the gas pedal and vroomed back up to highway speeds.

As she wove in and around cars, something wet dripped onto her upper lip. She snatched a tissue from the leather holder strapped to her passenger sunshade, thinking it was just a runny nose from allergies or from suppressing tears.

Blood. Panic and dread licked through Winter's body. "Not now. Please not now."

But the headache was already coming on, like a razor wire pressing into the back of her skull. Her eyesight grew wonky, and she knew from many years of experience, it wouldn't be long before her "gift" overtook her.

With a growl of frustration, Winter veered to the shoulder of the road. The pain of an oncoming vision drilled into her head. She put the SUV in park and squeezed her eyes shut. Then, as if she were a fish caught in a net, the vision ripped her away from her body.

Sometimes, she floated through the scene like a ghost. But today, her feet touched ground, buried in crunchy, dried-up leaves.

She lifted her chin to find a forest all around her. The branches were all naked, like at the end of autumn, when the last leaf had fallen but before the first snow.

Real nature was rarely so in sync.

That confusing and almost embarrassing feeling of walking into a room, only to stand there dumbfounded, crept over Winter. She was looking for something, but what? Her brain was drawing a useless blank, but her gut said to run.

She kicked her feet into action, not knowing where she was going, just that she didn't have much time.

"Winter!" Her husband's voice called out, weak and distant.

"Noah!" Winter ran harder through the naked trees, following the sound.

She burst into a clearing, and there he was—on the ground with a knife protruding from his gut as blood trickled from the corner of his mouth.

Frantic and numb, she stumbled closer.

Before she reached her husband, Winter was falling and spinning, falling and spinning. The bare trees bloomed with flowers, but no matter which way she tumbled, Noah remained hidden.

She ran back into the forest, and the branches with the blooming flowers clawed at her. Winter struggled. She tried to scream. "Noah!" *she finally managed to yell.* "Noah, I'm coming!"

Thump, thump, thump.

Winter stirred in her seat, jerking upright to get away from the claws.

Her eyes flew open, breath catching painfully in her lungs. She was back in her Pilot, blood dripping from her nose onto her lap.

Thump, thump, thump.

Flinching at the noise, Winter turned to find a man with a hard hat and sunglasses peering into her cab. She pressed the button to slide down the window.

"Ma'am, you can't park here. This is a construction zone."

Winter snatched another couple of tissues and pressed them under her bleeding nose. "I'm sorry. I was just feeling a little lightheaded."

"Are you okay?" The construction worker took off his sunglasses, revealing kind eyes caked in dust. "What happened?"

"Migraine." She wiped her nose and checked her reflection in the rearview. That was a choice she immediately regretted. Her pale skin was blotchy from tears, her nostrils caked with dried blood, her blue irises wreathed in red cracks like shattered glass. Even her black hair looked tired.

Winter glanced to her right, where a number of objects had colonized her passenger seat. Her office and home were so well organized, yet her vehicle always managed to look like a hoarder's den.

She snatched up a granola bar left there from a few days

ago and opened the wrapper. "Just need to get my blood sugar back up."

Worry clouded the man's features. "You gonna be okay? You want me to call somebody? Your husband?"

The suggestion was a sharp knife to her gut. "No. Thank you." Winter took a bite of the granola bar and put the SUV in drive. "I'm feeling better now. I'll get going."

The man looked unsure, but he took a step back, and Winter pulled back onto the highway. After stuffing the tissue up her nose to stop the bleeding, she gripped the steering wheel hard with both hands. She didn't have the wherewithal to worry about visions of claws right now. Not until she was with Noah.

Still, her sense of foreboding grew with every mile marker. She called him again and again. He'd said he was going to the hardware store to pick up more gizmos for their home and office setups—to prevent Erik Saulson and anybody else getting anywhere near either building without them knowing. He also mentioned his back was feeling tight, and he might go for a jog.

If he was out running, he wouldn't answer his phone. Maybe this was all nothing. She was panicking for no reason. Noah often went hours without looking at his phone—he was just that kind of person. He'd probably be wearing his smartwatch to track his steps and his heartrate, but he'd never set it up to receive texts or notifications.

"I get enough noise from my damn phone. I don't need a watch chirping at me too."

Noah was fine. He had to be. And in a few minutes— when Winter burst through the door and her big teddy bear of a husband looked up at her all confused—she would laugh about this.

They were going to laugh. Together. Over sandwiches.

3

Noah's truck was in the driveway when she got home. Winter was almost dizzy with relief as she pulled up next to it and tried to force tension out of her shoulders. But her jittery stomach refused to cooperate.

Leaping out of her SUV and not caring whether she closed the door or not, Winter raced into their house. She darted through the kitchen, where she noticed a few plastic shopping bags from a hardware store on the counter. Beside that were Noah's key and his phone, with his worn leather wallet open beside that. All his cards seemed to be there, but no cash.

"Noah!" Her voice cracked, a most unpleasant noise. "Baby? Answer me!"

She raced up the stairs to their bedroom. He wasn't there, but his jeans and socks lay neatly folded on the bed—what Noah did when he changed out of his street clothes and into his jogging clothes.

Winter raced back down the stairs to the front door, to the hook where Noah always hung his hydration pack. It was empty, and his bright-green running shoes were missing.

Setting a hand on the counter, Winter allowed her rigid, jittery body a moment of respite.

There was nothing strange about the state of the house. Noah had gotten back from the hardware store and decided to go for a run before getting started on the installation. He was addicted to running every single day. Even if a blizzard raged outside, Noah had to get his run in, or he got ornery. And half the point of running, at least for him, was to get away from the pressures of modern living.

Running was his thinking time.

Over and again, Winter tried to convince herself to calm down. Noah went for a jog. Nothing bad had happened. Nobody had been in their house, and there were no signs of a struggle. Noah would come through that door any minute now, looking happy and exhausted, like he always did when he returned from a run.

She tapped her fingers on the counter in quick succession. Again, she told herself he'd be back soon. Noah was dawdling because he didn't know about the voice message Saulson had left. He didn't know about the pictures.

Winter ran back outside to her Pilot and snatched up the pictures. She flicked through them—all the ones where Saulson had drawn a target on her with a red marker—until she came to the one of Noah.

The photo had been taken a few days ago. He was sitting on a bench at the park near her office. That was where he'd met a little boy who'd gotten separated from his mother, as well as some guy named Erik, who claimed to be helping the mother look for her son. Together, Erik and Noah made sure the child and mother reunited before going their separate ways.

The story should've meant nothing, except that Cybil had confirmed Noah's realization.

"Erik," Noah echoed before releasing a string of curses. "The man in the park. My height, beard? Crazy eyes."

Cybil looked past Winter to Noah. "Oh, yeah, that's him. But he's not your height. He must've had those dumb boots on with the heels. Thinks he's so clever. He did say he made a point of running into you. Said he wanted to look into the eyes of the attack dog before he put it down for good."

It was Erik Saulson at the park that day. Was the whole thing planned? Had the little boy been planted there so Erik could get close to Noah? Winter made a mental note to ask him if the boy was lost at the park before he got there. If Noah showed up first, it was a setup.

"Said he wanted to look into the eyes of the attack dog before he put it down for good." Cybil's phrasing echoed in Winter's mind. She squeezed her eyes shut, trying to breathe in through her nose and out through her mouth.

Definitely a setup.

Saulson was laughing at them. She took out her phone and opened the voice message again. The picture trembled in her hand as she pressed Play from where she left off.

"And I killed Opal. And I'll kill you, too, when I'm good and ready. Don't try to rush it, bitch, and don't you dare try to stop me. You've got a lot of leveling up to do first."

Once again, Winter stopped the message playback. Saulson had killed Opal—the aunt Winter just recently learned existed. She heard something odd in his voice near the end there, when he got excited and his volume and rate of speech sped up. Maybe it was just psychosis.

"Erik Saulson." Winter said the name out loud, letting the phonemes roll around in her mouth and through her brain. She'd already looked him up in every program in her arsenal, but his name was so common…

Even knowing how he spelled his first name would've narrowed the search, but she didn't know if he spelled his name with a *C*, a *K*, or both. Or maybe he preferred the German spelling, with a *C* and an *H*. Maybe he was using a pseudonym, and Saulson wasn't his last name at all.

This isn't helping. Focus. If I were Noah, where would I go?

If Noah went for a run, he'd be relatively close by, especially because they'd planned to meet at the house for sandwiches. BLTs, he'd said. To have those ready at noon, he'd come home any minute now to start frying the bacon.

Well, she couldn't just sit there and watch the clock, so she got into her SUV and fired up the engine, thinking she'd circle a few of the nearby blocks.

Once she found Noah, she'd insist he have his phone on him 24-7 from now on—at least until Erik Saulson was behind bars.

Winter pulled out onto the road and started down Noah's most common jogging route. She'd drive around until she found him, until he was in her passenger seat, his arms wrapped around her—until she could finally take a deep breath again.

"Noah!" she called out the window, but the wind swallowed his name.

She forced a laugh to calm herself down. Noah was fine. He had to be.

4

Special Agent Eve Taggart took off her blue-light-blocking glasses and dropped them on her desk with a gigantic yawn. The glasses reduced the eye strain of staring at a computer for hours on end, but this morning, they weren't helping. Neither was her triple-shot espresso.

Her four-year-old son was going through one of those phases where he refused to sleep unless someone was in the bed with him.

Jackie usually got up with the kids during the night, since he worked at home and could squeeze in naps from time to time. But he'd been suffering from a cold the last few days and had shot back some cough syrup before crawling into bed. Come midnight, when Alex went looking for Daddy, not even a nuclear bomb could rouse the snoring man. Mommy took the hit and didn't sleep another second all night.

Still, it was nice to get some extra cuddling in. She tried to remind herself, as her mother constantly scolded her, that one day she would miss being woken in the middle of the night by her baby boy.

With another leonine yawn, Eve got up from her desk and stretched her shoulders.

Feeling wistful, she glanced at Noah's empty desk. Falkner said she'd be getting a new partner in a few days—some woman transferring in from Alaska. Eve hoped they'd get along.

The intercom on her desk phone beeped to life. "Taggart?"

"Yeah?" she said through yet another yawn. She picked up her empty coffee cup and drank the black slime at the bottom.

"A woman is here to see you. Winter Black-Dalton. She says it's urgent, but she only wants to talk to you."

Eve tossed the cup into the trash can, her brow furrowing. "Is Noah with her?"

"No."

"Okay. I'll be right down." Eve snatched up her fitted black blazer from the back of the chair and pulled it on. The rest of the building was freezing compared to her little corner, where she had a space heater going most days. One nice thing about Noah leaving was she could crank up the heat again without having to listen to him bitch.

She closed the door as she left to keep the heat in and made her way toward the entry. What the heck could Winter want? Eve was friendly enough with her ex-partner's wife. She was Noah's favorite topic of conversation, after all. Eve probably knew a lot more about her than Winter realized. But she couldn't recall engaging Winter in conversation without Noah present.

It could mean only one thing—Winter was there to talk to her about Noah—which gave Eve a sinking feeling.

"Please, for the love of chili con carne, say he didn't cheat on her." She stopped and laughed at herself. "No. This is

Noah we're talking about. He worships Winter. He's literally obsessed with her."

She passed Agent Sizemore in the hall, and he quietly laughed at the way she always mumbled to herself. "What's up, Taggart? Your friends talkin' back yet?"

"Better company than you, shithead."

Eve slapped his upraised hand in greeting and kept on her way, her gaze trained five feet in front of her on the basic white tile.

"If she thinks he cheated on her, she's just straight-up wrong. No investigation needed."

When Eve walked through the locking double doors in the lobby, her attention went straight to the only person standing in the waiting area. Winter Black was beautiful even in a pair of nondescript slacks and a gray blouse with her hair pulled into a ponytail.

She rushed toward Eve. It was immediately obvious from her flushed skin and red eyes that she'd been crying. Blood tinged the edges of a nostril, and a few drops had dried on her shirt.

The sinking feeling in Eve's gut caught on fire.

"Winter?" Eve moved closer, the rubber soles of her Doc Martens squeaking lightly on the tile. "What happened? What's wrong?"

Winter shook her head hard. Her hand extended—shaking and so pale, it looked frozen. Between two fingers, she held a white kraft envelope.

"Noah's missing." Her words were a shaky thread of sound. She swallowed hard and cleared her throat. "I can't find him. I think something terrible's happened."

Eve took the envelope and slid the contents into her hand. There were several photographs, but the one on top was of Noah on a park bench...with his eyes scratched out.

Her heart skipped a beat. Winter's distressed face only

made it worse. Seeing anyone tremble and cry thick tears was painful. Watching former special agent Winter Black-Dalton do it was downright frightening.

"There's blood on you. Is it yours?"

She nodded and wiped her nose with a tissue from her pocket.

"Come on." Eve touched Winter lightly on the upper arm. She flinched, and Eve withdrew her hand. "Come back to my office and tell me what happened."

She swiped her ID to pass through the double doors. Winter followed in silence.

When they reached her office, Eve stood back to let Winter go in first. "Have a seat, okay? I'll be right back."

She jogged out the door, weaving around a few oblivious pedestrians before reaching her boss's office. Through the open door, she spotted SSA Weston Falkner seated at his desk.

"Weston?"

He didn't look up. "Yes?"

"I need you."

"Why?" He picked up a pen and scribbled something at the bottom of a page.

"Winter Black is in my office saying she can't find Noah."

His head jerked up. As a man in his mid-fifties, his skin was thick and weathered, white hair buzzed short to his scalp. He drew himself up from his chair to stand head and shoulders over Eve, his sharp blue eyes focused. He did up the buttons on his suit coat and followed Eve across the hall to her office.

Winter had not sat down. Instead, she'd pressed herself into the corner opposite the door and was staring at Noah's empty desk. She looked like a frightened rat hiding at the back of a cage. Eve wanted to hug her so badly it hurt, but

Winter had flinched just a moment ago, so she kept her distance.

"Okay." Eve snatched up her tablet and stylus. "Tell us what's going on."

Winter nibbled on her fingernail and pointed at the envelope on Eve's desk with the other hand. "Those pictures were on my windshield this morning."

Eve sat down at her desk and poured out the photos, arranging them on the surface so everyone could view all of them at once. Winter and Noah looked like they were out for a night on the town. They definitely didn't seem to know they were being photographed. Every picture was focused on Winter, and in every single one, a target had been drawn over her in red marker. All except one—Noah alone on a bench with his eyes scratched out.

"Do you have any idea who sent these?"

"I know exactly who sent them." Winter gritted her teeth, her eyes wild. "Erik Saulson."

Shit.

According to Cybil Kerie, Saulson was the puppet master behind Carl Gardner, the man who planted cameras all around Winter's office to monitor her every move.

When Noah went on sabbatical, Eve had made one thing clear. She told him she wouldn't use FBI resources to help him solve his wife's P.I. cases, no matter how nicely he asked or how much he begged. She also told him not to try to pump her for information on any of the FBI cases she was working. She was done sticking her neck out for him and his crazed vigilante wife.

But the Carl Gardner case was an exception. After Noah took that man down with a bullet, Eve promised to keep working the case and keep him informed on all developments. She was determined to do everything she could to track down Erik Saulson and anybody else involved in his scheme.

"He sent me a message as soon as I picked up the pictures." Winter took out her phone. Eve noticed how her fingers shook as she hit Play.

"Your baby brother left some pretty big shoes to fill." Saulson's voice trembled with excitement. *"I've read everything there is to know about him, and challenge accepted. But you're not like Justin. You still seem to think it's worth fighting on the losing side. He tried to show you, but you've been lagging behind, grinding away, building up your pointless little life. But I'm going to show you the good side of being bad. I promise."*

The voice faded to silence.

Eve swallowed the lump growing in her throat. Since she'd started working with Noah, she'd gone out of her way to learn the details of the Justin Black case. Everybody knew it, of course, but really sinking her teeth into the details and going behind the headlines had given her a fresh appreciation for why Noah was so very protective of his wife.

"Send me the recording," Eve said.

Winter nodded. "After I saw the picture of Noah on the bench, I went home to find him, but he wasn't there. He'd left his phone and his truck. His running shoes were missing, so I thought he was out for a jog. No big deal. We were going to meet at home for lunch anyway. High noon. BLTs. But I've looked everywhere for him. And he hasn't come home. And the man's timely if he's anything." Her lips trembled. "He's gone."

"Is it possible Noah took a different route than usual?" Falkner's cool voice gave nothing away. Noah had disliked him when he'd first come to work at the Austin offices, but they'd grown on each other over time. For her part, Eve would've trusted Falkner to lead her through a desert for forty years, though she definitely would've complained a lot.

"I'm not sure."

Falkner held his hand up. "Just to play devil's advocate, maybe he just went for a longer run to clear his head. Noah didn't know about the photos or the voice message, so he has no reason to think you might be worried, so he wouldn't be going out of his way to contact you."

A jolt rushed up Eve's spine, driving her to stand and pace the short length of her depressing little office. "Noah and Winter have been dealing with this stalker stuff for too long. He knows better than to go MIA for any period of time."

Winter nodded, her gaze following Eve as she paced. "Exactly. He'd never ghost me. He knew I was planning on coming home from work soon. That's why he suggested the sandwiches and said he was planning a quick jog first. If he was going for a long one, he would've said so. He wouldn't have offered to make lunch."

"How long has it been since you were last in contact with him?" Falkner ran a finger under his shirt collar.

Eve ducked under her desk and shut off the space heater.

Winter glanced at the big schoolhouse-style clock on the wall. "Almost two hours now. Honestly, if your wife had gone for a two-hour-long jog, are you saying you wouldn't be worried? Even if you hadn't received a threatening voicemail and found this on your car?" Winter jabbed her finger at the scratched-out eyes on Eve's desk.

"If my wife went for a five-minute jog, I'd assume she'd lost her mind or was taken by aliens." Falkner shook his head. "But I see your point."

"Winter's clearly in danger too." Eve tapped her stylus on her knee. "We should put a security detail on her, don't you think?"

"I think that sounds like the sort of thing we ought to talk to PD about."

Eve shot Falkner a cold glare and mumbled quietly enough that nobody could hear her say, "Bureaucratic pain in my ass." Turning to Winter, she returned her voice to conversational levels. "I'll keep an eye on you, then, and I'm going to make this my only priority until Noah's found."

Falkner looked irritated but nodded in agreement. "It's yours."

"Given the connection to the Carl Gardner case," Eve continued, "I'll get in contact with the digital forensic team and see if they've pulled anything new from his computer."

"Noah met him that day at the park. When Erik Saulson took this picture." Winter waved the photo in the air. "He didn't know it at the time. Noah described him as a man with a beard and crazy eyes."

"Send it to me." Eve clicked the button to wake up her printer. "Do you conceal carry?"

Winter lifted the hem of her pants to show an empty ankle holster. "Left it in my glove box."

"Good. Keep it on you at all times. And keep your wits about you. Until we know what happened to Noah, you and me are in a war zone."

"But listen, he's evil. And I'm concerned about police involvement. I'm just afraid…" Winter looked like she couldn't say the words.

Eve understood, and it appeared Falkner did too. She didn't need Winter to remind her that Erik Saulson had killed before and might do so again. Noah's life was top priority.

"Okay. The police need to know, but they're going to have to play it safe. Undercover when they're out in the field." Eve fixed her with a stern gaze. "I want you to check in with me every hour. Set up an alarm on your phone and shoot me a text, letting me know you're okay. Before you go to sleep, I want you to text me, and with what time you expect to wake up. When you wake up, I want another message. If you're going somewhere, I want to know where and with who."

Winter sighed, her shoulders drooping.

"If you don't text me, I'll call you. And if you don't answer, I'll hunt you down like a dog."

"Sheesh." Winter ran her hand over her face.

"Noah would never forgive me if I let something happen to you while he's gone. Until we find him, and he's back in action, I'm your overprotective husband. If I don't know where you are and who you're with, I'm going to worry. You don't want me to worry, do you?"

Winter nodded, her eyes glistening. "I'll check in. I promise."

"Thanks, babe."

5

Winter poured every ounce of faith she could muster into believing Eve would do everything she could to find her husband. Noah trusted Eve, so Winter trusted Eve. Simple as that.

Even though he was on personal leave, Noah was still a federal agent. That meant the FBI had jurisdiction over his abduction. But Winter wanted as many hands on deck as she could possibly get. After leaving headquarters, she made the short trip a few blocks away to the police station to alert local law enforcement about the kidnapping of a federal agent.

As she parked her Pilot and rushed into the station, she hoped Detective Darnell Devenport, her regular contact in the department, had come back by now. He'd been subpoenaed to New Mexico to help with the case of a man best known as the Railroad Killer, who traveled on old lines like a vagabond and performed B and Es at every stop, sometimes catching the homeowners in the process and killing them. Once the trial in New Mexico was over,

Davenport would bring the suspect back to Austin to stand trial in Texas.

Winter knew these things always took longer than it felt like they should, but she still said a silent prayer for his return. Working her last case with Detective Lessner as her man on the inside had given her an appreciation for Darnell and his endless snark.

"I think he's flying back in tonight," the uniformed officer tending the front desk said. "He's expected back at work by tomorrow afternoon. Would you like me to take a message?"

Winter drummed her fingers, noticing how ragged her nails had become. In her worry over Noah, she must've been chewing on them. She hadn't done that since she was a kid. It brought into sharp relief just how helpless she currently felt.

She clenched her fists until the knuckles turned white. She couldn't afford to lose her shit right now. She had to be strong, determined, professional. For Noah. Once she had him back and Erik Saulson was behind bars and this whole insane fiasco was at an end…only then would she give herself permission to truly freak out.

"This is urgent." Winter rolled her shoulders. "I need to speak with a detective now."

Footsteps sounded behind her, accompanied by a gruff, droning voice. "What seems to be the problem this time?"

Winter turned and found herself eyeball-to-eyeball with Detective Harlan Lessner. His computer bag was draped over his shoulder, and a paper coffee cup occupied his hand as if he'd just stepped into the office. As always, his expression was unpleasant—a mix between dejected hangdog and junkyard dog. Angry and unhappy about it. Or was it the other way around?

"Do you have something new on the Toler case?"

Winter silently accepted her fate. Without Darnell, she was stuck with this guy. He was a veteran like the other detective, though he'd only been with the Austin PD for about three years. She felt like a kid whose favorite teacher was out sick and had been replaced by everyone's least favorite substitute.

She shook her head. "No. It's my husband. I believe he's been kidnapped. He's Federal Agent Noah Dalton, and I came here straight from the FBI."

Lessner glanced at his coffee cup before eyeing Winter again. His frown somehow deepened, the furrows in his cheeks intensifying. Then he sighed and addressed the officer behind the desk. "I'll handle this." He waved for Winter to follow him.

Winter balled her hands into fists to keep her nails away from her teeth. She knew in her heart that Saulson would still be watching her, one way or another. Even here in the police station, his eyes were like lasers boring into her skin.

But that was ridiculous. She was safe here. Her frightened brain was becoming irrational. It was like part of her was underwater. Intellectually, she knew why. She was incredibly stressed, emotionally reeling, and trapped in a triggered state of fear.

In Lessner's cubicle, Winter sat in the chair beside his desk, steeling herself. She refused to give Saulson or anyone else the satisfaction of watching her crack.

As Lessner settled into his chair and woke up his computer, Winter's gaze wandered around the cubicle and back to that picture of him and his wife beachside. Even the second time, the photo seemed odd. Him in those long sleeves, arm around an attractive, bikini-clad woman, smiling without a care in the world. Where'd that guy gone?

With one hand on his keyboard and the other on his coffee, Lessner lifted his bulbous nose to her. "Tell me what happened."

Blinking back tears, Winter took the pictures from her

satchel and slapped the one of Noah onto his desk. "Erik Saulson left this on my car."

"This is the same Erik Saulson who allegedly partnered with Cybil Kerie?"

"Who else?" Her teeth clenched in irritation. No wonder people were consistently frustrated with cops—the way they asked obvious, pedantic questions, no matter how urgent the situation.

"Sure, sure." Lessner sounded like he was indulging an eager child who'd just scribbled a picture in crayon.

Winter pushed aside her irritation. "He left me a threatening voice message about playing a damn game with me. He also said he killed Kerie and my aunt and plans to kill me. When I got home, Noah was gone. We were meeting there for lunch. It looked like he'd gone out for a run, but it's been hours since we connected. He's not answering me and didn't show up for our lunch date. This is completely out of character for him. The FBI is on it, and we wanted to cover all our bases."

Lessner scratched the back of his neck. He was dressed in a tweed suit with a thin necktie. As usual, sweat beaded on his forehead. It was warm in his little square, and Winter rolled up the sleeves of her blouse.

"Little early for kidnappers to be out."

Anger popped in Winter's skull like cocking a gun. "Excuse me? They're not vampires, Detective."

"Right. Never mind." Heaving a great sigh, he leaned over his desk to root through his computer bag. He snatched out a small, stapled bag from a pharmacy and ripped it open. From inside, he pulled out a tube of something and narrowed his eyes at the tiny words printed on the label.

The son of a bitch wasn't even giving her his full attention. She had a flash of a fantasy where she picked up his framed photo and broke it over his balding head.

"I understand why you're upset, given the phone call and the photos. It's all very disturbing. Is there not still a chance this might just be a coincidence? Noah might come jogging back home any minute now."

First Falkner and now Lessner.

"Do you people think Noah does a fricking Ironman every morning?" Winter clenched her teeth hard to contain all the other angry words she wanted to spit at him. So many times, the shoe had been on the other foot—back in her FBI days when she was forced to feed the victim's families meaningless platitudes until she had a chance to dig into the case. Both sides of this particular desk truly did suck, and there was very little anyone could do about it.

"He hasn't called me." Winter wiggled her phone at him. "If he'd come home, he'd see the place is a mess. He'd pick up his phone from the counter and listen to all the frantic voicemails I left him. After all that, can you think of one good reason why he wouldn't call me?"

Lessner grunted. That was the closest to acquiescence she could expect from him or any officer of the law. They tended to be grunt-y people.

Besides, she'd rather be wrong and look like a fool than be right without doing everything she could to get her husband back.

"This is all related back to my brother. Saulson said so himself. I've been dealing with Justin and his cronies all my life." Heat burned in Winter's cheeks, creating tears in her eyes and fury in her fingertips. "Saulson said that my baby brother left big shoes to fill."

He unscrewed the cap on the little tube and used his fingers to smear some ointment on the back of his neck. "Do you know what that means?"

She was surprised he didn't already know, and the question was like a sucker punch to the gut. Unfortunately, there was no ambiguity on that point. "My brother is Justin Black."

"Justin Black…" His eyes flashed with instant recognition. "As in *the* Justin Black? The Prodigy?"

She cringed at the horrible moniker. "I've learned over the years to never take anything to do with him lightly."

"Naturally." His eyes stayed wide—the first time she'd ever seen him make an expression that wasn't exhaustion or vague disappointment.

She kept glancing at that beach photo, trying to make sense of it. The grumbling man sitting before her seemed to have virtually nothing in common with the trim, smiling husband in the photo.

"Black's such a common name. I guess I just never made the connection." He looked genuinely impressed for some indiscernible reason. "No wonder you seemed so calm in the face of everything that happened with Cybil Kerie. You must have some incredible stories to tell."

"*Incredible* is not the word I'd use." She couldn't help the feeling that he was lying about not knowing who she was. The man was a detective, for crying out loud, and they'd been working together for over a week. There wasn't a shred of a chance he hadn't googled her and fallen down the same blood-soaked rabbit hole everybody else always did.

What an ass.

"I'm not here to gab about my brother. I'm here to find my husband."

He leaned back in his creaky chair with a grandfatherly moan. "Seems to me you think those two things are connected."

"Justin's in prison. Erik Saulson's the one who kidnapped my husband." She closed her eyes, calling to mind everything Noah had said about Saulson. "He went up to Noah in a park and spoke to him the other day. He's about six feet tall, Caucasian, beard. Crazy eyes."

Lessner's lips had parted to say something when his phone buzzed with a text. He pulled out his phone, frowning hard at the screen. He typed something back. "Look, I know you like to work with Davenport, and that'd be just fine with me, except he's still wrapped up in the Railroad Killer case. I'll get everything started for you, I guess."

"Thank you. And Noah's old partner, Special Agent Eve Taggart, is also working the case under SSA Weston Falkner. You should coordinate with her."

"Great. I love a kitchen stuffed with cooks."

Winter was struck by the very specific urge to reach across the table, snatch him by his hair, and bite his face. She chewed on a fingernail instead.

"You should probably stay with family or friends until this blows over." Lessner balled a fist and rested his cheek against it, looking bored and tired. He scratched his wrist absently before grabbing his ointment and applying it there. "Getting involved in the case will only exhaust you and make our job more difficult. You're too emotionally invested to be of much use."

"If your wife was kidnapped, would you stay out of it?"

He glanced at the picture. "You never know just who you'll be after the hammer falls." His gaze met Winter's. "But, no, I would not stay out of it."

"Well," She exhaled the smallest sigh of relief at his response, "I've been dealing with falling hammers my whole damn life."

"I can imagine."

"Okay, then, Detective Lessner. But there's one thing. I've been warned about trying to stop him. Kidnappers always want no police involved. We can't treat this like a typical missing persons case. We have to canvass the area on the down-low, or Noah's safety could be…compromised."

His eyes narrowed into slits. "Now you're telling me how to do my job?"

Winter swallowed hard. "He's a soulless killer."

Lessner pursed his lips. He seemed to be considering her words at least. "Okay, I understand. Let's stay in touch."

With a short nod, Winter got up from her seat and left his cubicle without another word.

6

At times, fried chicken was my only joy in life. No matter what happened, who I disappointed, or how horribly shitty every other moment of my life became, I could always count on those eleven herbs and spices to stay true.

I sat in a tiny, two-person booth right near the buffet bar. Most franchises didn't do the buffet anymore, which was why I always made the extra fifteen-minute drive across town to come to this one. I noshed on mac and cheese and sipped my Pepsi, my phone in my free hand scrolling through old articles about the man I'd kidnapped and his enigmatic wife.

For a long time, I'd known Erik was after someone—a woman. And though he tried to be cagey about her name, Erik worshipped Justin Black, and he'd identified this mystery woman as a recent Texas transplant. It didn't take a brain surgeon to put it all together.

Still, I kept my mouth shut until recently, when he told me to kidnap Noah Dalton, FBI agent. It sounded nuts, and I told him so. He didn't care. Instead, he went off on some rant about Noah's wife, Winter, and I really couldn't tell if Erik hated her or loved her—though that distinction wasn't as important as people often thought. The opposite of love wasn't hate. It was indifference. I ought to know.

At first, Erik tried to be all mysterious about everything. I guessed he thought he was being slick, doing cool spy stuff. It wasn't my place to tell him he sounded like a tool, but I had to wonder what kind of adult man with self-respect would stoop to using code names. He was embarrassing himself and didn't even know it, the dumbass.

The last time we'd spoken, Erik called himself the Watcher and referred to his other partner as the Listener. His dead partner. And I was the Hunter. Lucky me.

The guy thought life was a video game. I suspected a lot of people out there were like that. The game absorbed them until they neglected their real lives—their health, their relationships, their finances. Erik was different. He brought the game into the real world.

I'd spent most of the last eight years of my life being crushed by misery and a belief that my life was already over. Erik changed that. He reminded me that no story was over until all the characters were dead. And he showed me that I had a lot more power than I'd ever realized.

The game wasn't over yet. It had only just begun.

I hadn't believed him—not until I wrapped my hands around Willa York's neck and finally, after so many years, administered real justice for what she'd done. When I choked that bitch to death, I could finally see the truth all around me. That was three months ago, and the feeling still lingered.

No matter what happened or how things ended between me and Erik, I would always be grateful to him for that. That was why I overlooked his juvenile tendencies. He reminded me what it was like to have agency again.

I picked up another piece of chicken and bit into it, the

grease coating my chapped lips as my burner phone buzzed in my bag. I set down my regular phone to check it. Only one person ever contacted me on that line.

A text message had come in, addressed to the Hunter, with a list of instructions on what to do with the *package*.

I shook my head. That guy. Everything he said was so Hollywood. He was lucky I didn't care about anything anymore. If he'd tried this stunt with me ten years ago, I would've destroyed him.

I didn't work for Erik Saulson. We'd made a deal. He was a silent partner in my grand scheme, and I was the same in his. It made him happy to feel like I was a puppet, so I let him. He didn't know I knew his real name, though.

Naturally, I let him think I was deceived by his pseudonym. Let him think I was just a clueless lackey doing whatever he said. This strategy was useful in my line of work —to be underestimated. That way, when shit inevitably hit the fan, my shirt stayed clean.

I was a man with nothing left to lose. Erik Saulson pointed that out. I often wondered if he had the good sense to be afraid of the monster he'd awakened inside me.

I sure as hell was.

Wiping grease from my fingers on a paper napkin, I read his ridiculous list of bullet points. Kidnapping an innocent victim wasn't the problem. I was fine with that, but Noah Dalton was not your average man on the street. Subduing the brick shithouse of a Marine in broad daylight without getting caught or leaving behind a trace of evidence had been no easy achievement.

Well, almost no trace. He'd lost a shoe.

The FBI agent had a squeaky-clean record. His most recent case had involved rescuing innocent children from an international human-trafficking ring. He was one of the good guys—somebody I actually respected. I'd agreed to kidnap him because Erik said that was all it would involve. I didn't have to hurt him.

Granted, I'd hit him with my car, but only because I had no other choice. Otherwise, he'd kick my ass before I could even get a tranquilizer into his system. But I never planned on seriously hurting him.

And now, Erik was changing the game. Worst of all, I knew none of this had anything to do with Noah Dalton. This was about Winter Black. What exactly Erik's vendetta was about, I hadn't a clue, though I suspected it had something to do with her infamous brother. But he'd helped me feed my need for vengeance. No one had ever done anything like that for me, and I felt alive for the first time in years.

Still…

No, I texted back. *That wasn't part of the deal.*

Waiting for his response, I reached for a chicken leg. I had already worked over it once, but there were still some good bits clinging to the bone.

There went those three little dots, bouncing beside Erik's code name on my screen. In my phone, I'd listed him as the Watcher like he'd asked, just in case he ever wanted the phone back.

If you want to learn the name of the other person responsible for turning your little girl into a speed bump, you'll do as I say.

I dropped my chicken.

Another name? What the hell is he talking about?

Rage ballooned in my chest. I remembered the visit from the police that day, the way the officer's voice choked when she told me Quincy had been killed.

The driver was Willa. Willa York. They ran a breathalyzer on her and found she was perfectly sober, just distracted. Just a self-important bitch who took a corner without looking.

Quincy had been at the crosswalk with Jackson—the dog

my wife took when we divorced. She packed that little guy in, along with my other child, my dignity, and my will to live, and off she went. Quincy had done just what I'd taught her, pressed the button on the crosswalk to set off the little yellow warning lights.

But Willa York had ignored those lights and hit her dead-on. My little girl died right there in the street.

Willa had shown remorse, but I knew that was only because she'd gotten caught. Her family paid for a fancy defense lawyer, so even though Texas was a *throw the book at you* kind of state, she'd paid a $5,000 fine and received a sentence of two years—and all but six months of that sentence was suspended because that little brat was a minor at the time. That was what my wife and I were supposed to accept as justice for the death of our little girl.

When that worthless bitch stood up in court and apologized for her crime, I'd never wanted to kill someone so badly in all my life. Erik was messing with the wrong guy if he thought he could play me with his lies.

I texted him back immediately.

Screw you and your BS, Erik.

His response came a moment later. *Someone else was there. Someone drunk. Someone who was driving but fled the scene so their name wouldn't appear in the police report.*

My blood pressure hit the roof as those eleven herbs and spices crept the wrong way up my esophagus. I was gonna be sick.

How the hell do you know that? If he was lying, I was going to tear that weasel limb from limb.

Drunk people like to talk. The stupid bastard told me himself.
Yeah, right.
I can prove it.
How?

I have video evidence. Complete the list...and I'll tell you what I know.

No. Evidence. Now.

I drummed my fingers on the table as I waited for something I was sure didn't exist. But to my surprise, a video came through a minute later.

I got up, dumped the rest of my food in the trash, and went to my car. Whatever was on that video, I wasn't watching it at some fast-food joint.

Getting in the car, I turned on the engine, cranked the AC, and pressed play.

Erik was bending the truth about one thing. The video didn't show who was driving the vehicle that killed my little angel. The freak hadn't uncovered evidence that was eight years out of date. But some drunk guy was blubbering on, stating, *"Willa told me not to drive"* and *"Some little girl with her dog"* and *"died shortly after impact."*

The snippet ended.

The facade of okay-ness that I cobbled together daily crumbled, and I was cannonballed right back to the worst day of my life. Swallowed by misery. My chest grew so tight, I wanted to tear my skin off to release the pressure. I punched the steering wheel instead. And again. And again. And again, until the bone in my hand ached, and tears pushed their way from my eyes down my face.

If my daughter's real killer was still out there, I was all in with this creep.

And he was out there. I believed the video evidence.

I'd already kidnapped Dalton, for crying out loud. But that crime was an afterthought, a blip on the radar, compared to the murder I'd already committed—compared to the crimes I was willing to commit to get justice for my little girl.

Once I identified this other driver—and left him as dead

as Willa—that was when my nightmare would finally be over. And maybe I'd be able to live again.

I leaned back on the headrest and closed my eyes, breathing deep in and out of my nose. I had to get my heart rate down so I could focus.

What the hell was she thinking? Who the hell had she been protecting? *Big mistake, there, Willa. One you paid for dearly.*

Once my daughter was truly avenged, I could start another chapter, even if that chapter was simply to die in peace.

When my wife divorced me, I didn't care that she'd always felt so lonely at home while I was constantly working, my desk buried in paperwork.

But I would've given anything to watch my little girl's ballet performance or walk Jackson with her one more time or go play on the monkey bars at the park she used to love.

Marcy left me because she and the kids were a "low priority." And then my angel died. After that, Marcy moved here, to Austin.

Nothing was worse than a lazy deadbeat who didn't take care of his family. Except a workaholic. Apparently, that was worse.

No man can win.

I followed her here a few years later, but since then, I'd only seen my son a handful of times. Marcy made it clear I wasn't welcome in his life, or hers, or the life of my son's new stepfather, the man he now called Dad.

How ironic that she left me for not being there, and now she hated me every time I tried. I hated her, too, as a wife and as a person. But I also loved her because she was Quincy's mother.

I watched two flies dancing in the air as they buzzed in front of my windshield. After all these horrible years, I was finally going to do right by my daughter. Complete what I started.

I guessed I had to be grateful to Erik Saulson for that.

The clock was ticking.

And I had work to do.

I'm in, I texted him back and peeled out of the parking lot.

7

Noah woke to a splitting headache. His first instinct was to struggle, but he forced himself to stay still until he could figure out his situation. Vague memories pooled in the back of his brain, hinting at what happened moments before he blacked out.

He got home from the hardware store and had started installing new cameras when he realized he'd bought the wrong size mount. Standing at the kitchen counter, he'd cursed himself, knowing he had to go back. He'd made himself a slice of toast with a banana and some coffee with collagen peptides. He didn't want to eat too much because he planned on having lunch with Winter.

The store was only two or three miles away, so Noah decided to kill two birds with one stone. There was space enough in his hydration backpack for the mounts. He'd jog there, buy the part he needed, jog back, get the house all set up, fry the bacon for sandwiches, enjoy lunch with his beautiful wife, and head to the office to beef up security there.

He was not going to lose Winter again. If he had to take

out a second mortgage to pay for private security detail, that was what he'd do. Nothing in the world was more important than keeping his wife safe.

After changing into shorts and special moisture-wicking socks, Noah had laced up his shoes, set his fitness tracker to record the run, and thrown on his pack. Then he grabbed a couple of twenties from his wallet to pay for the mounts and headed out the door.

He remembered sucking in a breath that left the scent of peach blossoms in his nostrils. Now, mid-April, the trees were bursting into bloom. Both a blessing and a curse. He loved the scent, but Winter's allergies had worsened since their move from Richmond to Austin—a different species of ragweed or something. Who knew?

He decided to swing by the pharmacy across the street from the hardware store to pick up some nasal spray for her —or she'd suffer through the whole season with watery eyes and a leaky nose.

Noah was rounding a blind corner—a six-foot hedge blocking most of his view—when a car careened into sight and struck him head-on. He reacted by rolling onto the hood, trying to protect his legs from shattering. His chest and torso took most of the impact, knocking the air from his lungs. He would have survived the impact just fine if he hadn't fallen to the asphalt so hard he smacked his head.

Even though he'd seen stars, Noah had already drawn himself up to his hands and knees by the time the driver exited the car. He was about to turn around and yell for them to watch where the hell they were going when something struck him hard in the back of the skull.

Now he was here.

But...where was here?

A jab of panic pierced his aching skull again, but Noah did not react to it. Bronze sunlight peeked through a slit in some blackout curtains. He hadn't been unconscious for long. Or at least, it didn't feel that way.

The space registered as small and heavy, a musky and distinctly human scent in the air. He wondered if he was in a small apartment until he noticed the aisle leading from where he lay, past a tiny kitchenette and toward a windshield.

An RV. That meant he could be anywhere.

Noah wiggled his hands and feet, testing the restraints holding him in place. His wrists and ankles were wrapped and strapped individually—four limbs tied to each of the four corners of something. A bed frame, possibly. Though that made no sense. A four-poster bed frame in an RV?

A wave of nausea rushed over him. He turned his head to the side, neck creaking, and took a deep breath through his nostrils. Since there was a gag in his mouth, he was relieved he didn't puke. He shifted and cringed at the pain in his ribs. Damn car must've fractured them. His left arm ached, too, especially the shoulder joint, which he could tell was horribly swollen. Sharp pain shot down his fingers.

He was so thirsty.

As long as I'm alive, I'm okay. Noah had said these same words to himself many times. *I can get out of this. I just need to focus.*

His thoughts ran naturally to Winter, wondering if she was okay or if whoever had come for him had come for her too. Between the gloom in the RV and his limited angle, she could've been lying unconscious on the floor, and he wouldn't know. The place seemed cluttered, with clumps of shadow in every corner.

Thinking of her in danger was even worse than thinking about his own situation. For the sake of survival, Noah forced himself to push all unnecessary thoughts from his brain.

Remember your training.

As a Marine, he'd been through so much, including capture-specific survival tactics. SERE—Survival, Evasion, Resistance, Escape.

The Code of the United States Fighting Force, designed to guide members of the armed forced who had been captured, was not written for civilian situations.

"I am an American, fighting in the forces, which guard our country and our way of life. I am prepared to give my life in their defense."

True enough, but unhelpful. He scrolled forward in his brain.

"If I am captured, I will continue to resist by all means available."

That part translated nicely to civilian situations.

What were his available means? He was strapped down and spread-eagled. All that was missing was a Bond villain with a laser pointed at his crotch.

I am a U.S. Marine. I am never without resources. I am the fucking resource.

First, focus.

Noah closed his eyes again and took in another slow breath—though he kept this one shallow to spare his cracked ribs. He listened to his pounding heart and focused on the exhale.

To the panicked animal mind, breathwork was the ultimate trickery. When he breathed slowly, he told his lizard brain that it had been misled and he wasn't about to die, so it could calm down and let him think straight.

Observe.

With his heartbeat steady and his wonky stomach momentarily soothed, he opened his eyes again. He was in the back of a small RV, strapped upon a mattress that was elevated on a makeshift bed frame. His limbs were secured to what seemed to be the legs of a dining table turned upside down.

Outside was deadly quiet. He couldn't even hear the sound of traffic. The RV was somewhere outside the city, but it couldn't have gone too far. Noah hadn't been out more than a few hours.

His ribs were cracked, his left arm twisted and swollen, taking it out of commission. He wiggled his wrists, feeling the make of the straps. Leather, like a belt.

Plan. That's the next step.

The leather bands holding him down were tight. His odds of working his way out were slim. He strained against them, testing the yield in each strap. Almost nothing.

A wave of torment surged through his chest. Maybe his ribs were worse off than a fracture or two.

Envision.

He closed his eyes again and tried to imagine the person who'd put him here. He hadn't seen the driver of the car. Hell, he would've been hard pressed to say what color the vehicle was. It had all happened so fast.

There was only one suspect in his head, though—Erik Saulson. The man who'd been stalking and tormenting Winter for weeks now. He'd used Carl Gardner to set up cameras at her office. He'd used Cybil Kerie to send out fake flyers for her business, getting Winter tangled up in all that. And then, when Winter and Noah came for Kerie, Saulson swooped in on her as she fled and finished her off.

The man was merciless and intelligent. Not to mention obsessed.

Noah tried to imagine him walking into the RV, tormenting him. In the calm, focused, and observing state Noah had lulled himself into, he tried to come up with scenarios in which he could overtake his captor, but they all came back to the same basic point.

Saulson would have to untie him first. Noah was too wounded, his binds too effective, for him to break free. Everything ached except his ribs—sharp pain shot through them with every breath he took. And his mind was awash with heavy gray clouds, likely from drugs and maybe a concussion too.

And he was so thirsty. Every time he swallowed, needles embedded themselves into this throat. His hydration pack lay on a nearby nightstand, which only made it worse. This all led him to one infuriating conclusion.

There was nothing for him to do but wait.

8

Winter didn't buy it for a second, but just in case Lessner was right and Noah's disappearance had a less sinister explanation, she called every hospital in Austin. He'd be wearing his dog tags—he always wore them—so it would be simple enough to identify him even if he were incapacitated in some way.

Nothing. She gave every hospital administrator she spoke to Noah's full name and a detailed description. She even faxed along his picture, just in case.

Just in case.

She was making herself sick with all her contingencies and possibilities.

Before heading home, she drove along every possible jogging route she could think of, rolling down every street at a snail's pace as she carefully scanned every bush and every inch of concrete.

She wasn't even really looking for him anymore. She knew he wouldn't be there. She was looking for something else—a sign of where he'd been.

Why couldn't her visions ever tell her something useful,

like where her damn husband was? What was she supposed to make of a forest full of naked trees that spontaneously started to bloom and tried to scratch her skin off?

Her head was throbbing. She pulled into her driveway beside Noah's truck, Lessner's advice echoing through her head. She ought to stay with family until Noah came back and the whole thing blew over. Her stomach lurched at the idea of trying to sleep in their bed without him.

She went inside to pack an overnight bag. One shirt, one pair of pants, one pair of socks—that was all she'd need, because she would find Noah tomorrow. She had to.

Winter returned to her SUV just as a nondescript sedan rolled past her house with a nondescript forty-something guy in plainclothes at the wheel. At least the cops were searching and being discreet. On her way to her grandparents' house, she tracked Noah's possible jogging route again, where she passed a government issue SUV. That would be the Feds.

When she pulled into her grandparents' driveway, Winter noticed all their lights were off. She checked her watch. It wasn't even nine yet, but she knew they went to bed excruciatingly early. Still sitting in her Pilot, she texted Eve, letting her know where she'd be spending the night.

Eve texted back that every agent and officer in the state of Texas was looking for Noah.

Seeing it with her own eyes and hearing it from Eve, Winter felt more hopeful than she had all day.

She grabbed her overnight back and dragged herself along the path toward the door. After knocking and trying the knob, she leaned against the doorjamb and waited. It was a good five minutes before her grandma opened the door. She was dressed in her old housecoat and pajama pants, her wavy white hair pulled back in loose bun.

"Winter?" Gramma Beth reached forward and clasped her on the shoulder.

The gentle touch made her muscles tingle with electricity. Her face grew hot, and though she tried to hold it back, all at once, Winter started to cry.

"Oh, my goodness, sweetheart." Gramma Beth shuffled outside and wrapped an arm around Winter's waist, guiding her inside. "What's going on? What's the matter?"

With snot leaking from her nose and a gooey lump at the back of her throat, Winter spilled everything. She told her about the pictures, the phone call, and the clues she'd found in the house. As she spoke, Gramma Beth led her to the living room and settled her on the corner of the couch. Winter cried every stinging, gritty tear she'd been holding back all day.

Her grandmother held her tightly and smoothed her hair. After a while, her grandfather appeared at the top of the stairs. He looked grumpy until his eyes found Winter's. His face softened, and he hurried his large frame down the steps to sit beside her and hold her shoulders.

"Can I stay here tonight?" Winter lifted her eyes to both of them in turn. "I can't go home and be alone. I just can't."

"I'll get the guest room ready." Gramma Beth grunted as she rose to her feet.

"You're going to need your sleep, honey." Her grandpa handed Winter another tissue. "I'll get you one of my knockout pills."

"No. I couldn't. I—"

"I'm not gonna let you spend the whole night tossing and turning, driving yourself crazy, and then send you out in the morning looking like death. Get yourself a good night's sleep, and we can all start fresh in the morning." He stood and shuffled to the medicine cabinet in the kitchen. From her spot on the couch, Winter just saw the back of his head and his leather slippers on the white tile.

Winter leaned over her knees. "I can't be drowsy. I have to be sharp."

"Exactly." He came back with one very tiny yellow pill and a glass of water. "Take it, honey. You look like hell. You need sleep. I promise, I'll wake you up bright and early. And if you need an upper, I got those too."

She laughed weakly and buried her face in her hands. Her grandpa was becoming a veritable pharmacist in his old age. She worried about feeling like death in the morning, but the idea of being knocked out for a few hours and getting a respite from her crippling anxiety was too seductive.

She took the pill. Forty minutes later, she was blissfully unconscious.

❄

Winter was surprised by how spry she felt the next morning. Grampa Jack's pill had given her no dreams and left her with no ill effects. By five she was up, and by five thirty she was fed, showered, and ready for the day.

Except she'd forgotten her toothbrush. And the special conditioner she used to keep down her incorrigible flyaway hairs. Oh, and her polarized sunglasses that Noah got her last Christmas to wear during fieldwork.

Not to mention Grampa Jack only had decaf coffee. *"The caffeine runs right through me,"* he'd told her when she'd complained about it before.

Before six a.m., Winter was behind the wheel of her Pilot. Last night, she had nearly despaired. Now, with a new day gearing up, her hope renewed

On the drive home, Winter found herself wondering if

she ought to call Noah's mom to let her know what had happened or if that would just worry her unnecessarily. He would be found soon, so there really was no reason to get the poor thing upset. Noah's mom was a very sweet woman, but she had a tendency to overreact. Winter wasn't sure she could deal with any more emotion right now.

Tomorrow. If she didn't find him by tomorrow, then she'd call. But she'd find him today, so it was a moot point.

Her phone dinged as she pulled into the driveway, but her gaze was glued to the white envelope taped to her front door.

Her heart tightened like clay in a mold. She killed the engine and drew her Smith & Wesson from her ankle holster. Checking to make sure it was ready to fire, Winter slipped out of the cab. She scanned the area, running through a mental checklist of hiding places, before finally making her way up the stoop.

If only Noah had gotten the cameras installed, she would've been able to review footage of whoever had put the envelope there.

It had to be Saulson. Or maybe a new crony of his. It seemed that was how he preferred to operate—like he fancied himself some kind of general on the hill, sending out his troops against the enemy.

Winter didn't take the envelope. Instead, she unlocked the dead bolt and slipped inside. Room by room, she secured the location, checking every window and interior door to make sure they were fastened. She grabbed Noah's spare set of keys and pocketed them. There was nothing she could do to guarantee Erik Saulson stayed out of her house, but she could make it harder on him.

Pausing in the kitchen to grab some latex gloves, Winter went back to the front porch and peeled the tape back from the envelope. Then she caried it inside to the kitchen counter. The envelope flap was merely folded under, not sealed.

Winter opened it and turned it upside down. An object fell out and struck the counter with a metallic ting, a piece of paper sailing softly behind it. Looking down, her heart stumbled.

The object was a ring—a simple band of Damascus steel, acid etched to show a stylized tree line like winter reflecting in water. Her eyes fogged over as she studied it, remembering the day she'd bought it, and the way Noah's eyes had lit up like a little kid when she gave it to him in a box with a green ribbon.

His wedding band.

Winter picked the ring up and clenched it tightly in her fist.

Her phone rang, and she jumped like a startled cat. She almost ignored the call before she remembered the promise she'd made to the caller herself.

"Eve, I got another letter." Ice coated her throat. "He sent me Noah's wedding ring."

Eve's voice was hard. "Where are you?"

"Home." Winter put the phone on speaker and set it down on the table.

"Are you alone, Winter? You shouldn't be alone right now. I'm coming over."

Winter unfolded the letter that came with the ring. It had an unremarkable font, something wide. Courier New, probably.

"'Congratulations,'" she read out loud. "'You have reached Level Three. To continue your quest, go to your place of business and wait for a New City friend whom you've never met. Help her find her treasure, and she will lead you to the prize you seek.'"

Pure, unadulterated rage surged through her veins.

She forced herself to finish reading. "'PS, be careful who your friends are. People with badges must not be trusted, unless you like having dinner with rats. FBI headquarters and Austin PD are out of bounds. And every time you go out of bounds, the prize will be charged a penalty. Sincerely, the Watcher.'"

She wanted to throw the letter across the room and shoot it. She didn't, because that would be insane, but dealing with Erik Saulson and his games was propelling her closer and closer to that line.

Which was what he wanted. Winter would not give Saulson the satisfaction of driving her mad.

At some point, the phone line had gone dead. She inhaled to a count of four, paused, and exhaled to a count of six. She still felt murderous, so she did it all again, inhaling for four, pausing, and exhaling to a count of six. She repeated the cycle until a knock came at the door.

"Is that everything he sent?" Eve didn't bother with formalities as she walked over to examine the evidence on the counter. "The ring and the warning about bringing in law enforcement?"

Winter nodded, her brow wrinkling as the words ricocheted through her skull. Saulson was threatening to hurt Noah if she went to the cops, obviously. A pretty standard move kidnappers pulled to try to cover their asses.

Eve's nostrils flared. "He's screwing with you."

"'Dinner with rats.' Is he saying he has someone in the police working with him?"

"He'll say whatever he can to try to isolate you from the people he knows can protect you."

In the corner of the letter, Winter noticed some numbers handwritten in pencil—*2591414*. She turned the paper over, examined the envelope, and looked at everything under a black light she brought out from a drawer. There was nothing more.

She spoke each number out loud, turning the sequence over in her mind. "What the hell does that mean?"

9

The last thing Winter wanted was to waste time sitting around in her office, but she didn't feel she had a choice. The letter very clearly stated what the next portion of her "quest" would involve—a New City friend she'd never met. She had no idea what his riddle meant, but something told her she might be getting a new client soon.

She wondered vaguely if Saulson himself might show up, but that seemed out of character. More likely, he'd send a crony.

Saulson was clearly skilled at coercing others to do his bidding, even when it exposed them to so much potential danger. Both Carl Gardner and Cybil Kerie were dead as a result of their connections with Saulson and the things he talked them into doing. And in Cybil's case, he'd pulled the trigger himself. So far, Winter knew Saulson was good at collecting cards to play against others. Blackmail, bribery, and who knew what else. Murder, apparently.

Her gut tightened, thinking of the young woman who'd thrown her life away for the sake of revenge. Saulson had found her pain point and used it to manipulate her.

Winter had liked Cybil. Even for all the innocent people she'd hurt, she still hadn't deserved what happened to her. She belonged behind bars, but because of Erik, she was serving eternity in a pine box.

Her cell phone rang. It was Eve. Winter glanced at the time and realized she was four minutes late on her check-in. In her defense, she'd just seen Eve a few hours ago.

"Hello?"

"Where's my text message?"

Winter rolled her eyes. This was going to get annoying quickly. "I'm still alive. Any news on your end?"

"Your neighbor two houses down, a Mrs. Beverly Gorse, saw Noah leave your house in jogging attire at ten-thirty or so yesterday morning, headed west. She was the last person to see him." Eve popped her gum, making Winter cringe.

"Okay." Winter peered through the glass wall of her office that opened up to the street, though she wasn't really looking at anything. "That narrows things down a little. Anything else?"

"I spent all night scouring the internet for Erik Saulson with any connection to Cybil Kerie or the other victims."

Winter thought about chewing a fingernail or two. She forced herself to keep her hands away from her mouth. "Did you find anything?"

"I'm staring down at a great big pile of nothing. I thought since we know he was headed southwest, maybe I could get you to sketch out a few likely jogging routes for him, and then I can check the CCTV."

"You got it. I'll do it now and email you."

"Perfect. How are you holding up?"

She twirled Noah's ring around her thumb, watching the shiver of light in the steel. Use of her personal forensics kit had lifted no prints, so she hadn't bothered sending the ring for testing. That might count toward more law enforcement help than she could get away with anyway. "I don't know."

"I can't believe he keeps sending you riddles. It's like he wants you to catch him." Eve popped her gum again. The woman chewed louder than an overworked dad in a nineties sitcom. "And what's with all the *Final Fantasy* crap?"

"*Final Fantasy?*" Winter looked at the letter again, which she'd placed in a baggie that lay on the desk before her. "You're right. He talks in video game lingo."

"Clearly, this neck beard thinks he's the smartest person to ever live. I bet if you met him in the wild, he'd tell you his IQ and SAT scores while you lit the fire from rubbing two sticks together."

Winter almost laughed at that. She enjoyed thinking of Saulson as a neck beard. "This isn't the first time he's mentioned this 'game' he and I are supposedly playing."

Eve sighed. "Now that he's admitted to kidnapping Noah, I don't think you have any choice but to play along. Every game has rules. If you follow them, maybe we can keep Noah safe until we can get him back."

"I don't know what his damn rules are." Winter tested Noah's wedding band on her thumb to make sure it fit snugly. She'd keep it there until she could slide it back onto his finger, where it belonged. "Don't talk to the cops, I guess. Though he made it sound like that was for my sake."

"Do you really think there's an LEO working with this scumbag?" Eve popped her gum.

Winter pulled the phone away from her ear for a moment. "Whether there is or there isn't, Saulson's a talented little investigator. Or at least, he knows how to get talent to do work for him. He probably already knows I went to the FBI and the police. He might've been following me all day."

Eve made a sound like an exaggerated shiver. "Creepier

than a centipede crawling through chocolate pudding on your tongue."

Winter scrunched up her nose at that image.

Noah had mentioned on more than one occasion that Eve could be a little odd—and not only because she liked to hash out her cases by having full-on conversations with a synthetic bamboo plant named Pokey. Still, Winter hadn't been quite prepared for Eve the Crime-Stopping Investigator in live time.

"That's not untrue." Winter was about to say more when she noticed a woman step up to her office door. "Hold on."

In her early fifties, with short black hair styled into perfect vintage curls, the woman was dressed in a smart houndstooth skirt suit and led a minuscule chihuahua by a tiny pink leash.

"I think the New City friend I've never met might be here."

"Be careful and keep your gun within reach every second. Call me after and let me know what happened. I'll get back to searching for the needle in Erik Saulson's haystack."

Winter hung up and rose to answer the door. The woman on the other side smiled politely, though she had one of those cold faces that seemed much more comfortable with a grimace.

Winter's gun was secured in a clip-on holster in the back of her pants now—where she always used to keep it when she was in the FBI and knew she might have to use it at any moment.

Nothing had really changed in that regard.

"Hello. Are you Winter Black, the private investigator?" The woman spoke with a neat and proper New England accent.

"Yes. How can I help you?"

The little dog jumped up on Winter's leg. Even on its hind legs, it barely reached the top of her boot.

"My name is Nancy York."

New City.

New York.

I guess this is my friend.

"This is going to sound a little unusual, but I received a letter in the mail telling me to contact you."

Winter lifted a brow, as though nothing about that sounded remotely unusual. "Come inside and have a seat, please, Ms. York."

"Nancy, and thank you."

Winter led Nancy back to her office and gestured for her to settle into the plush leather chair in front of Winter's desk, while she relaxed into the reclining roller. "It's my daughter, Willa." She reached into her purse and took out a five-by-seven posed shot of a young woman—à la JC Penny portraits.

The girl was maybe eighteen and pretty. Her black hair was pin straight and styled in a pixie cut. Her jean jacket, adorned with colorful cartoon patches, was straight out of *Saved by the Bell*.

"I just found out this morning that she's been missing for the last few months."

Winter had to inwardly control her eyes from popping out of her head at that comment. "Are you not very close?"

Nancy shifted uncomfortably in her chair. "We're both quite busy."

Clearly, she'd hit on a touchy subject.

"Oh, and she's in her mid-twenties now. That was from high school. Here." She held up her phone to show Winter a photo off a social media site.

"Can you text that to me?"

Nancy nodded, and Winter handed her a business card

with her number. "Have you gone to the police yet to report her missing?"

Shaking her head, the austere woman retrieved an envelope from her purse and promptly handed it over. "When I woke up this morning, I found this blank envelope on the stoop next to my morning paper."

Winter fetched a glove from the box she kept in a desk drawer and snapped it on before accepting the envelope. Stuffed inside were two sheets of paper. On the first was a screenshot of an article printed off the internet—a write-up on Cybil Kerie and what she'd done. Near the bottom, a single line was highlighted. *Kerie replaced Dr. Poole's previous receptionist, who went missing at the beginning of January.*

That line made Winter sit up straighter. She flipped to the second page. Typed lines, standard margins, Courier New font. Just like the letter Saulson had sent her. Winter read the note out loud. "'Your daughter has been missing for several months, and you didn't even notice!'"

Though Winter had entertained that exact thought only a few seconds ago, she'd had no plans of voicing her opinion. So much for that.

She read the next sentence. "'Never fear! Detective Winter Black is here!'"

This was followed by her office address and phone number. She flipped the paper over, checking the corners for numbers.

Nothing. Well, that certainly explained the office visit. "Tell me more about Willa. Is she the person mentioned in the article? Dr. Poole's previous receptionist?" That couldn't be a coincidence. To say she was curious was an understatement.

Nancy picked up her tiny dog, moved her purse to the floor, and set the wee thing on her lap, petting her head so that with each stroke, her big, weird eyes bugged out.

"She'd been with Dr. Poole a year or so, I believe. Or was it two?"

Ay yi yi.

"And when did you last speak to her?"

"Over Christmas." She lowered her gaze to the dog. "Willa and I do not have what you might call the closest relationship."

"Could you point me toward someone who might've been closer to her?"

"I'm sorry, no. I don't know any of her friends." Nancy delicately lifted her shoulder. "I did call her landlord, and apparently, she moved out of her apartment, also three months ago. You might try talking to Dr. Poole."

It was rather arrogant of Nancy to presume Winter would take the case. Not that she was wrong. Between the note from Saulson and the connection to the Blue Tree Wellness Center, Winter was all over it. She just didn't appreciate the assumption.

"Can you give me your daughter's last known address?"

"Mm-hmm." Nancy grabbed pen and paper from Winter's desk, went into her phone, and scribbled out a few lines. "I'll also give you her phone number, though it doesn't work. I tried it after I got the letter. And here's my phone number as well. Can you please let me know if you find any information?"

"Of course. Call me if you think of anything else."

"Thank you so much for looking into this. How much is your fee?"

"I'll make a couple phone calls and see what I can find. We can discuss a retainer afterward. In the meantime, you should file a police report."

"Will do." Nancy nodded sharply and stood, glancing at the dainty gold watch on her wrist. "Thank you so much for your help. Good luck."

"Make sure you give the police the recent photo that you texted to me."

"I will."

Winter stayed at her desk as Nancy fled the office, her dog tucked under her arm. Something about the interaction didn't sit right, though Winter couldn't be sure if that was because Nancy was a liar and a sycophant for Saulson or because she was just a cold, narcissistic person and subpar mother. Either way, she gave Winter the creeps.

Like a centipede crawling across your pudding.

She shook her head, flipped open her laptop, and searched *Willa York*.

10

As I pulled up next to the RV in Winn Junkyard, I felt an ache in my throat. I didn't want to do this. Noah Dalton had never done me any wrong. In fact, he was the sort of person I'd always admired, back when life mattered.

I looked the guy up, hoping for dirt—anything that could justify what I'd agreed to do. I'd hoped to find some sketchy affiliation, some greased palms, or some willing participation in wartime atrocities. All I found was an all-American boy with morals and principles. A loving husband, a decorated Marine, a devoted agent.

Noah Dalton was a good man, and that made me absolutely sick. When I'd first joined forces with Erik, I knew it'd be a slippery slope. But hopefully one riddled with degenerates who deserved their fate.

Not this guy.

But I couldn't back out now. Not when York, the woman I'd spent the last eight years despising, was only partly responsible for what happened. She'd been in the car that killed Quincy. She'd allowed somebody else, somebody who was intoxicated, to drive. And as my daughter lay bleeding on the concrete, she'd let that other person get away.

I had no remorse for what I'd done to her. In fact, I had an out-of-control craving to do it again to the bastard who killed my angel.

The first moment I held Quincy and her teeny fingers wrapped around one of mine, I finally understood love at first sight. I'd cut off my arm to bring her back, so it followed logically that I would cut off somebody else's arm—or their head—to bring her justice.

But Dalton had nothing to do with any of it. And yet here I was, tasked with cutting off one of his fingers. I should've known that was next in the lineup when Erik told me to bring him his wedding band.

Fucking hindsight.

When this was over, I'd tell Marcy everything, and she'd know beyond a shadow of a doubt that I'd always loved her and our family. That our life together meant more to me than anything else. I had no fantasy that she'd take me back, but I wanted her to know.

Dammit. I wiped my face with my big, clumsy hands. "Don't worry, princess. I'll never give up on you. Daddy's going to make things right. No matter what."

Grown-ass man, crying in broad daylight. I needed to get my shit together.

I put on two pairs of gloves—one medium-sized that fit my hands like a…well. And then large-sized ones over that. Just in case something happened.

Next, I snatched up my sneakers from the passenger seat. I'd bought them to wear that night with Willa—the first time I'd purchased a special occasion outfit since my wedding. The shoes were two sizes too big, and the day before I went after Willa, I'd filed the tread pattern off with a hand sander.

I'd worn the sneakers to kidnap Noah too. I'd wear them

when I killed the driver who stole my little girl. Then, when I was done, I'd slide a couple of bricks inside them and toss them into a lake.

My coveralls from that night were already decaying in a landfill. A fresh pair sat in sealed plastic on my seat. There weren't very many products to which I was brand-loyal—fried chicken, mac and cheese, and disposable protective coveralls. Tyvek just made a superior product.

As I broke the plastic, I noticed how sweaty and cold my hands were. They were even shaking a little.

My mind roiled with images I'd found on the internet. Noah graduating from college with his proud mom at his side. Noah in uniform in a write-up in the *Richmond Times-Dispatch* for bringing a killer to justice. Noah and Winter at their wedding—laughing and so damn happy, it made my guts lurch.

I wondered, if Noah or Winter had been on the case, would they have figured out that Willa hadn't been driving and was actually protecting someone else? How hard would either of them have fought to get justice for my sunshine?

Balling both my hands into fists, I almost punched the steering wheel again. My heart was beating too fast, my breath puffing in and out like a damn steam engine. Erik was transforming me into a monster. I didn't even recognize myself anymore.

Bolt cutters sat on the passenger seat. I nabbed them, got out of the car, and slammed the door. Then I leaned against it, my body trembling.

"I can't do this," I cried, like a whiny kid. I kicked the car door hard enough to leave a dent and hurt my toes. "The hell I can't!"

Ashamed, I looked around, but it didn't matter. No one could hear me, except maybe Noah. The junkyard was all but abandoned. It was a real graveyard of car parts, smashed-up vehicles, and piles of old tires. Before kidnapping Noah, the only other time I'd come here was to dump Willa's car. Better that than some good Samaritan reporting her abandoned car in the woods. Wrecked cars belonged in the junkyard. Faded into the background. Disappeared the way I'd made Willa disappear.

Plus, there was this RV that Erik had strategically planted here.

If I didn't follow through with the task, the son of a bitch who killed Quincy would get away with it. I couldn't let that happen.

If Noah Dalton knew the story, he'd understand. Everything I'd read about him suggested he was the sort who'd sacrifice himself for a little girl. This was no different.

Bringing Quincy's killers to justice was the only thing that mattered. My life had been meaningless for so long. No more.

I set the cutters on the car roof and stepped into the Tyvek suit, tying up the hood so it covered my hair, not that there was much of that left. I put a double layer of surgical masks over my nose and mouth and goggles on my eyes.

Grabbing the tool Erik had so generously supplied, I turned toward the RV, and that was when I was seized by a horrible pain in my gut. I shouldn't have eaten right before coming here. The cutters shook in my hand.

What if Erik was lying? What if he'd fabricated the so-called video evidence? What if he didn't have a damn thing and was tricking me into killing, kidnapping, and mutilating people who had absolutely nothing to do with Quincy's death?

If that jagoff is lying, I'll hunt him down and break every bone in his skinny little body.

Though I was no Noah Dalton, I could still murder a weakling like Erik Saulson with my bare hands.

I looked down at the bolt cutters.

My hand would not stop shaking. My bones hurt. My flesh felt tight. My stomach roiled in revulsion, flavors from my lunch bubbling up my throat. I didn't want to do this.

Saliva pooled in my mouth, a precursor to vomit. I pulled down my mask to spit it out. I couldn't turn back now. We had an agreement. *If I handle this, he'll tell me what I need to know.* Once this was over, I could finally move on. My life could begin again. Or at least, it could end in peace.

I stepped up to the door, pulled the key out of my pocket, and stuck it in the lock.

My stomach really hurt. After all the effort I'd put in to keep from shedding bits of myself on the crime scene, it'd be a shame for me to vomit all over it and just spew DNA everywhere.

I didn't want to do this. Noah Dalton never did me any harm. Neither did Winter Black, for that matter.

But without Erik, Willa would still be alive. I owed him.

The burner phone dinged in the pocket of my coveralls. Erik, of course. I snatched it out and glared at the screen. Four text messages.

Your mission, capture the cuck.

Status, in progress.

New Task. Time attack. Slice and Send.

Ready player? GO!

It made me want to beat him when he talked to me like that. I stormed away from the RV and called him.

He answered before it rang even once. "Yes?"

"I swear, asshole, if you're screwing with me, I'm going to break every bone in your skinny-ass body."

"You're there, aren't you? With the cuck?" The little freak sounded aroused. "Have you done it yet?"

"I want a name. Now."

"Stop being such a bitch and just do it, bro. You know how this works."

"I mean it, *Erik*." I spat his name. "I'll break you like a pretzel. And then I'll cut *your* fingers off and feed 'em to you if you don't give me his name!"

"Mm-hmm, that's the Hunter I hired. Nice energy. Now go complete the mission, and you'll receive your reward."

"The name, Erik. Who killed her?"

"I got it right here, bro. I want to see proof of Noah Dalton's bloody ring finger severed from his body, and it's all yours. His ring is getting lonely, after all." He hung up.

That dude was one sick puppy. Annoying too.

I left the phone on the hood of my car and headed back toward the RV. Now or never. There was no going back.

As I turned the key and stepped inside, the door squeaked. A smell of urine bit at my nostrils. The man had been tied to the bed for more than twenty-four hours. The smell made me feel guilty, just a little.

Noah lay on a mattress at the back of the RV, strapped to four corners of a dining table I'd flipped upside down. The RV didn't belong to me, so I did what I could.

I stuck the key in the ignition and tested the cigarette lighter. It glowed orange.

I knew there was a first aid kit under the kitchen sink, so I took it out and riffled through the contents. Gauze, medical tape, a tube of triple antibiotic. Good enough.

"Who are you?" Noah's voice drifted toward me from the bleakness at the end of the little hallway. I could've sworn I left him gagged. He must've gnawed through it.

I needed to be very careful with him, make sure I left absolutely no opportunities for escape. If I gave him a single inch, he was gonna take a hundred miles.

As I stepped closer, I saw the strap still hanging about his neck—half chewed through and wiggled out of its place.

Son of a bitch. I'd known I had my work cut out for me, kidnapping a Marine.

Holding the bolt cutters in front of me, I approached and checked that all his binds were still in place.

Good. He'd only managed to get the gag out. But not good, as now that meant I had to listen to him. He needed water anyway. I grabbed his hydration pack—that water had to be a hundred degrees by now—and stuck the straw in his mouth.

He sucked it down like a man crawling through the desert. Which was good, as I didn't have any plans of killing the guy, certainly not by dehydration.

When he appeared to be done, I set the pack back down.

"Whatever you're planning, you don't have to do this." He stared at the bolt cutters. "You haven't gone too far yet. You can still end this. If you let me go right now, I promise I'll never try to find you or bring charges against you. We can just pretend this never happened."

Noah struggled against his restraints, though he must've known by now that was fruitless.

Fear will make a man take unreasonable actions.

I stepped close to him, knelt, and curled three of his fingers under so only the ring finger rested on top of the nightstand beside his makeshift cage.

He tugged his hand so hard, the screws creaked. "No. Please. You don't have to do this. We can work this out. Just talk to me."

I ignored him. Hardened my face and blocked him out. His words would only make this harder. I focused on his tan line from the wedding band I'd removed earlier.

For Quincy. For Marcy. For myself. I had to do this.

I wiggled his finger in place inside the bolt cutters.

"Please god, no. No!" He yanked back hard again, trying to thrash, but he was tied too tight, and he was still dehydrated and concussed. He had broken ribs and was sweating like crazy. His eyes…they were so glossed over. I had to stop looking at him.

No eye contact!

I readjusted his finger. "It's nothing personal."

He yanked it away again and curled his hand into a fist.

I opened it back up. "Stop moving! You really don't want me to miss."

I had to be fast. I yanked his ring finger back and into the cutters. Before I could think about it anymore, I clamped the cutters shut with both hands.

Snap.

11

A jolt of electricity raced through Noah's whole arm. The man in the white coveralls swore up a storm as Noah's severed finger thudded onto the carpet. With all that drama, he was acting like he was the one who had just gotten mutilated.

A moment later, Noah's brain caught up to the pain. What felt like lightning shot out in all directions, to his whole body, and then boomeranged back, settling into a sharp ache in his left hand. Screaming and thrashing, Noah could see spurts of blood squirting out the fleshy nub where his finger had been. The remaining nub was hot and horrid, though the cold air was ice on the open wound.

The man left his side. Noah couldn't be sure if he was still screaming or not. It was impossible to see beyond the red in his vision, and the pain was unlike anything he'd ever known. Even being stabbed in the guts by Timmy Stewart hadn't hurt so profoundly.

The man came back, snatched up his hand, and pressed something to his wound. The searing pain caused his whole body to lurch. He could smell something too. Sounds came from his throat and chest he'd never known he could make.

Fight! The word in his mind was a direct order. *Now's your chance!*

He yanked so hard on his wounded hand to escape from the pain that the table he was strapped to creaked and shifted.

Noah tried wrenching his hand into his chest. The leather cuff was still secured to his wrist and the table leg, but a splitting sound came from beneath hm. The pain in his finger was so all-consuming, it drowned out the pain from his fractured ribs, giving him his core strength back.

Fight! Do whatever it takes to escape!

The man pressed down hard with all his weight on Noah's left arm. He used all his strength to pull away, but the man held tight, falling over his chest. He lashed Noah back down like he was subduing a lion that had just been hit by a tranquilizer dart. He wrapped rope on top of the leather cuff, circling it around and around.

Tears were in Noah's eyes—tears that felt like blood. His vision seemed to work only in flashes and spurts. Noah saw his bleeding stub was now black and blistered. The full horror of what had just happened slammed down on him all at once. The sick freak had just cauterized his wound with a damn cigarette lighter.

Splitting the table had been nothing short of a feat of adrenaline. But it wasn't enough. Now Noah lay flat, his chest heaving, his body broken by the pain. His mind swam, reaching for unconsciousness, folding back on itself.

How he wished the blackness would just take him, even as the man wrapped his nub in gauze and secured it with tape.

But unconsciousness would not come.

After bandaging his wound, the man stood and stepped back. Steady footfalls padded across the floor after that.

Noah's head fell to one side, tears soaking into his hairline, his ear, and the mattress. The man returned with a bag. He picked up Noah's severed finger and stuck it inside, which looked like it was full of ice. Then he bent down and put that inside a cooler.

"I will destroy you." Noah's voice came out breathy and raspy. "You'll pay for this. I swear. I'll kill you."

Noah could see nothing of the man's face behind the mask and clear goggles, but he could tell he was staring at him.

"I doubt it." Without another word, he picked up the cooler and left, the click of the lock the only other sound.

Heart racing, Noah panted and trembled with frustration. He wanted desperately to give in to the darkness. He didn't want to be awake anymore, didn't want to feel the excruciating pain of being alive.

But his mind would not shut off.

Who the hell was this guy? He was too short and stalky to be Erik Saulson—or at least, it wasn't the guy he'd met in the park. Probably another of Justin's followers. Another pathetic loser trying to make something of themselves by clinging to The Prodigy's sickening legacy.

Or the man could be any number of gangsters Noah had pissed off over the years. Most recently, he and Eve had taken down a large ring of Mexican and American traffickers. This could be revenge for rescuing the last of their "product," arresting their main operators, and destroying the moneymaking machine they'd spent years building.

Could be...

Mercifully, his mind began to slow, and he fell farther and farther into the deep black ocean of unconsciousness.

His last hazy thought was of Winter—a prayer that she was safe and not suffering as he was.

12

As Winter walked through the manicured succulent garden that led from the parking lot to Dr. Poole's office, she waited for her new bestie to answer her call.

"Winter Black." Eve sounded happy to hear from her.

"Hey, Eve. I'm down at Dr. Poole's to interview her for this new case, the one Saulson wanted me to take."

"Deets?"

"The client is Nancy York. Her daughter went missing about three months ago. Until then, she'd been Dr. Ava Poole's receptionist for over a year."

"Remind me who Poole is."

"Dr. Ava Poole employed Cybil Kerie. Poole had an affair with Kerie's dad. As a result, the parents divorced, mom took her own life, and dad became an alcoholic who ended up wrapping a vehicle around a tree." Winter sidled away from a tall cactus with long needles that grew a little too close to the pathway. "Cybil Kerie set out to systematically destroy Poole once she met Erik Saulson on the dark web in a community for haters."

"Got it. So you think Willa York's disappearance is related to Saulson and everything else?"

"I think whatever happened to her was his doing, making it possible for Kerie to take York's job and get close to Poole."

"That doesn't sound like good news for Willa York. You think we're looking for a body?"

Winter paused just outside the door to Poole's office and took a deep breath through her nostrils. One of the cactuses, a prickly pear by the front door, had burst with tiny yellow blooms since Winter had last been here. She brushed the hairlike petals with the tip of one finger.

"I don't know. There's a decent chance." Noah's wedding band on her thumb winked in the sunlight. Winter closed her eyes. "I couldn't tell her mother that, though."

"Poor woman. What a shitty reason to die." Eve cleared her throat. "But on that note, anyone looking into immediate family? Love interests?"

"Nancy York promised to file a missing persons report. Assuming she followed through with that, the police will be on it too."

"Roger that. So when's the last time you ate?"

Winter wrinkled her nose. Had she heard that right? "What?"

"When did you eat last?" Eve repeated much slower this time.

For a moment, she genuinely couldn't remember. "Yesterday, I think."

"Right. After you talk to Poole and before you do anything else, you need to eat."

Winter set a hand on her trembling stomach. "I don't think I can."

"You have to. You need your strength. If your stomach is stressed, eat something simple, like a smoothie and some toast. Give me the address where you're at, and I'll drop something off."

"No. You don't have to do that." Winter gritted her teeth. "I can feed myself. I'm not a baby."

A sound like fingers clicking on a keyboard came through the phone. "Is this Dr. Poole of the Blue Tree Wellness Center?"

Winter smacked a hand lightly to her forehead. "Eve, no. I'm not going to let you be my personal Meals on Wheels. I'll eat. I promise. I just forgot."

"Do you have any dietary restrictions?"

"No, but—"

"Awesome. See you in twenty."

Before Winter could protest further, Eve hung up.

Though she low-key wanted to throttle the woman, Winter couldn't help but feel a flicker of affection for the overbearing pain in her butt that was Eve Taggart.

Breezing through the door into the office, Winter immediately noticed a young man sitting behind the sleek desk with its live bamboo front. Unfortunately, his glasses reflected the light from his computer, so she couldn't see his eyes. That was where Cybil Kerie had once sat, and Willa York before her. The thought made her stomach hurt even more.

Gray marble tiles squeaked under her boots. A burbling fountain of copper and stone faced a display of beautiful hand fans painted in muted natural colors. The air smelled of agarwood today, and Enya played gently over the speakers.

"Hello." The receptionist smiled. In his early twenties, he had a perfectly coiffed beard and luxurious blond hair that hung loose over his shoulders. "Can I help you?"

Memories of Cybil left Winter feeling wary of the young man. Could he be yet another plant from Saulson?

Stepping up to the front desk, Winter set a hand on the cool surface. "I need to speak with Dr. Poole."

"I'm so sorry, but she's not seeing clients today. She's participating in an online conference."

"Will you just tell her that Winter Black is here? I'm sure she'll want to talk to me."

The man jumped a little in his chair, knocking over a pen holder. "You're Winter Black?"

She pulled a very fake smile. "Ta da."

"Wow, I've heard everything about you and what you did for the doctor. You're one of her favorite people."

Winter was equal parts flattered and embarrassed. "That's nice."

"Go on in. She won't mind since it's you."

"Okay. Thanks." Under other circumstances, Winter might've questioned his logic and asked him to announce her anyway. But screw it, she was in a hurry.

She knocked on Dr. Poole's door and stepped inside. The doctor sat at her desk in full makeup, her hair styled. She was in the middle of a sentence when Winter stepped in. Instantly, she cut herself off.

"I'm so sorry," she said into her headset. "Will you all excuse me for one moment?" Clicking her mouse, she swept off the headset and rose to her seat. "Detective Black."

"Winter, please." Civilians liked to play fast and loose with *detective*, but to her, it just didn't sound right. Nothing sounded as right as Agent Black had. She probably just needed more time with her own P.I. firm.

"What are you doing here? Is everything all right?"

"Not exactly. Do you mind if I have a seat?"

"Please." Dr. Poole indicated a chair with her long, willowy arm. As she settled back behind her desk, she slapped her laptop closed.

With a deep inhalation, Winter informed Dr. Poole about

Willa York's disappearance and her suspicion that Cybil Kerie and her accomplice might've hurt her so that Cybil could take over the receptionist position.

"Could you tell me more about the circumstances of Willa's departure? Did she put in notice?"

Dr. Poole looked like she was trying to frown, but Botox was stopping everything but the very edge of her hairline from wrinkling. "No. It was a no-call, no-show. That sort of behavior wasn't unheard of with Willa, though she was a good employee when she came in. But it had gotten so frequent that I told her the next time she didn't call in to let me know, not to bother ever coming in again. That was right after the holidays. A few days later, I hired Cybil."

Winter knew good help could be hard to find. She'd gotten lucky with Ariel. A pang thudded in her chest as she thought about her assistant, who she hoped would be coming back to work soon.

"Willa had this boyfriend, a really charming fellow with all manner of attendant issues with drugs and alcohol."

Winter's backbone perked. "Do you know his name?"

"Richard Benderell, I think. Went by Rich. She used to talk about him a lot. It seemed to me he did nothing but make her miserable, but she was in love." The doctor sighed lightly. "In fact, she was a codependent, having grown up with parents who were both adult children of alcoholics. Her mother especially was a very cold woman. I believe they were estranged."

Leave it to a therapist to start talking about someone's mother, regardless of the question asked. Though in this case, she seemed to have hit the nail on the head. "Did you try to contact Willa after she didn't show?"

Dr. Poole nodded. "I called several times and left voicemails. Our policy when it comes to no-call, no-shows is to let someone go after the third time. That was Willa's eighth or ninth no-show in as many months. I sent notice of her termination via email by week's end."

That explained why Dr. Poole had not made more effort to track Willa down. The young woman had already proven herself unreliable.

Dr. Poole leaned back in her chair. "Come to think of it, I'd just finished leaving Willa the message about letting her go when I went to lunch at a nearby deli and ran into Cybil. I hired her on the spot, given our history. And she did pass her background check and drug screening after that, and I…well, I just didn't see it coming." Her head drooped.

Winter hated having to bother the woman after what she'd just gone through. She'd been framed for murder and locked in jail, and she'd lost three patients to an evil mastermind and his sidekick killer.

"I see you have a new receptionist." Winter needed to move on.

"He's a temp. I haven't been able to commit to hiring a new person full time." She twisted her hands in her lap. "Cold feet, I suppose."

Considering her last receptionist had tried to kill her, that seemed fair.

Winter took Dr. Poole through a line of questioning about Willa York. Most of her answers came back short and inexact. Clearly, they hadn't had much of a relationship outside the office.

She'd gotten pretty much everything she needed out of the doctor when a knock on the door startled them both. Winter looked over her shoulder as the door creaked open and Eve poked her head in with a cheeky smile.

"Delivery for Winter Black."

13

Eve dropped off Winter's lunch with a smile and very short lecture but didn't stay to chat. She'd delivered cauliflower cheese soup, a salad, a small baguette, and a large orange-and-passion fruit smoothie. It was a tremendous amount of food.

She had no expectation Winter would actually eat all of it, but there was enough variety for her to find something she could manage to choke down. She needed to keep her strength up and her mind focused. Food was a very important part of that equation.

Showering a person with food was the only way Eve knew how to express affection during a hard time. Her compulsive honesty wouldn't allow her to spout platitudes or vague offers of help. She much preferred to put her energy into making soup and baking bread when possible, though she wasn't above purchasing her food gifts from a deli case.

Focusing on taking care of Winter was the best possible distraction from her worry about her ex-partner and what might or might not be happening to him.

What might have already happened...

In truth, bringing Winter lunch was an excuse to get out of the office and swing by the police department. Winter had mentioned a Detective Lessner—who Winter had worked with on Cybil Kerie's case—was now looking into Noah's disappearance.

Erik Saulson had ordered Winter to keep the police out of things, but that seemed a ludicrous request, considering he'd just kidnapped an FBI agent. He was smarter than that, and Eve knew it. Still, they all needed to tread lightly. Until she had his neck under her boot, that was.

With a flash of her badge to the receptionist, Eve was led straight back to Lessner's desk. In her time at the Austin VCU, Eve had worked with a good number of police detectives. She had a sense that she'd met Lessner before, though her memory was patchy.

When Eve came up behind him, the detective twirled in his chair to face her and pocketed the phone in his hands. "Agent Taggart?"

"Detective Lessner. How you doing?"

He rose from his chair to shake her outstretched hand.

He was shorter than Eve—five-seven in her boots, with an extra boost from her high ponytail. He probably had a hundred pounds on her, though, with broad shoulders and thick, trunk-like limbs. His skin had the texture of an old citrus, and his flat black hair was slowly retreating from a tired forehead. He looked uncomfortable, too, like someone was jabbing a fork into his thigh.

"I'm here to follow up on Noah Dalton's disappearance."

"We don't have any news yet. We've got some unmarked cars circling the Destiny Bluff neighborhood, branching out for ten square miles. And we have one tailing Winter, per your request. We're vigilant but keeping it low-key."

"I just came from Winter, so I saw your people. Can I get

a look at your notes? I don't want to be retracing steps you've already taken unless I run out of other things to do."

He laid his arm over his desk. "We're a team, of course. I'll shoot 'em to your email."

Eve nodded curtly. "Perfect. I'll also need you to share a case file with me, a missing persons. Willa York."

"Missing persons?" Lessner's scowl deepened as he turned to his computer and tapped away on its keyboard. "Willa York…" His meaty fingers typed away. "Looks like it was just opened, though mom said she hadn't heard from her since…" *tap tap tap*, "the beginning of the year. What the…oh, and it says here she worked for Dr. Ava Poole…" he glanced up at Eve, "as in the Dr. Poole that I arrested for murder last week?"

Eve nodded. "And promptly released, yes."

Years of training and experience had taught Eve how to keep her mouth shut. And given Erik Saulson's threat that somebody in the force was working for him, she worried the police database was compromised. The fewer people who knew all the details, the better.

Noah would pay the price if they failed to follow Erik Saulson's rules. It made her so angry, she could barely see straight. Still, she took a deep breath.

"So that means Cybil Kerie took over her job?"

Eve nodded again, much happier to confirm information than provide it. "Yes, back in January. Willa hasn't been seen since."

"Cybil Kerie took over…" Lessner rubbed his chin in thought. His brow was furrowed like an angry bulldog. "You think Saulson got rid of Willa York so Cybil Kerie could take her place?"

"Or he got Kerie to do it herself."

"Fair enough." He shrugged and groaned, scratching at his neck. "I'll check with an officer in the missing persons unit and keep you informed on any developments. As of right now, there's nothing to share other than her mother's statement." He narrowed his eyes at his computer monitor. "I see Nancy York spoke with Winter Black before coming to us. Why is she still working on other cases right now?"

"She's not *working*. Like I said, she's trying to see if Willa York and Noah's disappearance might be connected."

"We've got a task force for this."

"Her husband is missing," Eve snarled. She caught sight of a picture sitting on the edge of Lessner's desk—him standing with one arm around a pretty redheaded woman, a goofy smile on his face. He looked like an entirely different man than the one in front of her. She wondered what story that picture told. A question for another day.

"Agent Taggart?" Detective Darnell Davenport poked his head around the cubicle wall.

The first thing she noticed was how tired he looked. The bags under his eyes nearly reached the bridge of his nose—so gray they looked black on his dark-brown skin. He was dressed in a gray slack suit under a tactical vest with a dozen pockets, holding everything from extra pens to his gun.

"You're here?" She rose from her seat and bumped his fist. They'd known each other for years, having worked together a half dozen times since she was assigned to Austin. He was a good man and a smart investigator, if a bit touchy and stiff at times. She also happened to know he was Winter's preferred contact in the department. "I thought Winter said you were out west."

"Just got back this morning on the red-eye. I'll probably have to go back out. It's a pain in my ass." He rolled his eyes before hardening his face with a scowl. "I heard about Winter's husband."

Eve's phone pinged.

It was a picture of the inside of Winter's car. On the

passenger seat, she'd laid out all the food Eve brought for her with a bunch of bites taken out of it. Winter held a half-empty smoothie in front of the screen.

Happy boss? She'd texted.

Eve hearted the picture and slipped her phone back in her pocket. "That was Winter."

"How's she holding up?" The softness in Darnell's voice was unmistakable. Even if he complained about Winter causing trouble for him all the time, it was clear he'd started to look at her as one of his own.

A lump caught in Eve's throat. The image she kept fighting to keep out flashed in her mind's eye—Noah's bloody and beaten lifeless body abandoned somewhere in the woods.

Eve clenched her teeth and imagined a giant's hand reaching into her brain, ripping the thought out, and throwing it away. It was not useful to think of such things, and utility was the name of the game in the Bureau.

"It's been more than twenty-four hours," Eve said. "We believe he's been kidnapped by Erik Saulson, the same man who's been stalking Winter and who recruited Carl Gardner and Cybil Kerie. She's been warned not to involve the authorities, and he's a known killer, so we're doing what we can without being obvious."

Darnell's weary face awakened with quick rage. "I'll handle the police side of this from here, okay, Harlan?"

Lessner shrugged and pressed his fingers into his temple, like he had a lazy sort of headache. "Be my guest."

The intercom on his desk switched on with muted static. "Detective Lessner? There's a delivery for you in the foyer."

He swirled on his chair and jammed down the button on the phone. "Be right down."

As Lessner got up and headed away from his desk, Darnell touched Eve lightly on the elbow and guided her across the aisle. "Tell me what you need. I don't have time or energy to get fully read in on this thing, but anything the police aren't doing, I'll make sure it happens."

Eve brightened, seeing in him an ally rather than a grudging assistant. "Willa York. She's a missing person. I need—"

"Say no more. I'll get you everything." Darnell rushed to his desk, Eve on his heels. His fingers moved swiftly across his computer keys, and a moment later, his printer whirred to life. Eve snatched up the hot papers as they came out and read through Nancy York's official statement. The detective in the missing persons unit had already solicited CCTV from the bar where Willa York was last seen. It was a start.

Eve had opened her mouth to ask Darnell to pull that up when it started playing on his monitor. She glanced at the picture of York in the report, reminding herself who she was looking for. Black pixie cut, skin like printer paper.

The footage was of an exit door—black and white, grainy, time stamped. Willa York had entered at 11:37 p.m. on January the fifth and left at 1:26 a.m. Both times, she was alone.

"No cameras inside the bar?"

"I don't know. There's been no movement on her credit or debit cards, and her phone hasn't been used since that night," Darnell said, reading off the report online. "They're looking at cell phone towers to see where she was last time her phone was used. I'll send a message to Detective..." he flipped through the papers, "Detective Smith. I'll make sure they know to keep you up-to-date on all developments."

"Thank you, Darnell." Eve stood to leave, slipping the printout under her arm.

"You're welcome." Darnell rubbed his tired-looking eyes. "But I don't know. This wasn't called in for three months. Three months. The odds aren't in York's favor."

Leaving Darnell's office, Eve was reaching into her pocket to grab her phone when she came around the corner and bumped right into Lessner.

He stepped back with a grimace. In one hand was a large soda and in the other a red-and-white fast-food bucket.

"Sorry." Eve sidestepped the smell of fried chicken skin and spices.

Instead of replying, he grumbled something under his breath and moved past her toward his desk.

14

Winter's stomach popped and groaned as she pulled up to the Haven House Apartments, where Willa York lived with her two roommates. Though Winter grudgingly acknowledged Eve's point about needing to eat, her gut was not pleased with her. Anxiety and food did not go well together.

"I'm back at the office now," Eve said over the speaker, after she finished telling Winter what she'd learned from Darnell.

Hearing that he was back in town was a breath of sweet air. She wouldn't have to go through Lessner anymore.

"I've collected a fair bit of CCTV along Noah's route, and I'm sitting down to review it now. Where are you?"

Winter set a hand lightly on her stomach to try to shush it. "I'm at Willa York's apartment. I'm going to interview her roommates."

"Do you want me to come?"

"I'm fine. You keep doing what you're doing. I'll give you a call when I'm done."

"All right, Winter Black. You be careful. And if anything smells fishy, get the hell out of there and call me, okay?"

"You got it." She clicked the button on her steering wheel to hang up and killed the engine. She almost felt like she was back in the FBI again, the way she was having to report in and keep track of her position. It was kind of nice. A sense of normalcy to ground her in the moment.

She exited the SUV and headed into the apartment building—six stories of gray stucco and uninspired mirror windows. The apartments were identical, distinguished only by decorations on the small corner balconies.

She didn't know if anybody would be home, but she wanted to get a look at the place. Besides, Nancy York had been unable to provide contact numbers of either of the women her daughter had lived with.

Exiting the elevator on the fourth floor, Winter walked down the stark-white hall to York's door and pressed the illuminated doorbell. Music was playing inside—something vaguely hip-hop.

After about a minute, a woman in her early twenties with long brown hair answered the door. Her eyes were a shade of blue not found in nature—almost certainly from contacts. "Yes?"

"Hello. My name is Winter Black. I'm here on behalf of Willa York's mother to investigate her disappearance. Do you mind if I ask you a few questions?"

The woman's big lips parted, and she set a hand on her chin. Winter noted the small, poorly executed rose tattoo vining around her pinky down the back of her hand and wrapping around her wrist like a garden snake. "Holy shit. I mean, are you serious? Willa's really missing?" She stepped back from the door.

Winter put one foot inside the place, leaning against the open door.

The apartment was larger than she'd expected, with a skylight in the tall ceiling of the living room. A chesterfield and loveseat were both made of pink leather.

Winter pulled out her notebook. "Can I have your name, please?"

The woman crossed her arms and dug her toes into the plush carpet. "It's Chelsea Gray. Gray with an *A*."

"Do you live here?"

"Mm-hmm. Me and Missy."

Winter decided to take advantage of Chelsea's cooperative attitude. "What's Missy's last name?"

"It's Stoder." She spelled it out.

"You seem surprised that Willa's missing. When was the last time you saw her?"

"Yeah. I mean, I knew she left. Like three months ago. But I thought she just stopped talking to us, you know? I kept thinking she'd come back to get the rest of her stuff, but she never did. I've texted her about it a bunch of times. But then it's like...I get it."

"What do you mean, you *get it*?"

Chelsea hesitated a second, her eyes darting. She wrapped her arms around her middle. "I figured she just didn't want to risk running into Missy. And she was pissed at me too."

"Why?"

"Well...she had this boyfriend, Rich Benderell." She spelled out that one too. "They broke up right before she left. I mean, like, that was why she left so quickly and left behind, like, her bed and her microwave and all her books and stuff."

"Why did Willa and Rich break up?"

Chelsea's neon-blue eyes wandered. Just then, another woman stepped into the front room. She was dressed in a black golf shirt and short skirt with a small apron, her hair tied under a black do-rag so only a hint of curls showed at the nape of her neck. She was tall and curvy with dimples so deep, they showed, even though she was scowling. "What's going on?"

"This lady is a detective," Chelsea said quickly. "Willa's gone missing."

The other woman looked at Winter like a fly in a wineglass.

"Are you Missy?" Winter asked.

"Yeah."

"I'd like to ask you some questions, too, if you don't mind."

Harrumphing dramatically, Missy looked at her watch. "Fine, but make it quick. I have to get to work."

"When was the last time you saw Willa?"

Missy thought for a bit. "It was on a Tuesday," she finally answered. "I remember, because Tuesday was her day to use the washing machine, and I asked her to do one of my dresses with her load. When she left that night, she took the load of laundry and my dress with her."

Winter quickly ran the timeline through her head. "So that would've been Tuesday, January the sixth?"

"Yeah, that sounds about right. It was just this cheap rayon dress, but it fit me like a glove."

"So Willa left in a hurry, is that right?" Winter shifted her gaze between the two women. "Do either of you have any idea why that might've been?"

Chelsea bit her lip and looked at Missy, clearly the dominant one in this relationship.

"Who the hell knows why Willa does anything?" Missy twitched her jaw from side to side, like she was trying to crack it. "She was a manipulative bitch who lied and played on everyone's emotions to get what she wanted out of them. She's probably not even missing. She's probably just trying to get attention."

Clearly there was no love lost between Missy and Willa.

And both of them clearly knew exactly why Willa left when she did. "Who's she trying to get attention from?"

"Rich, of course. Who else?" Missy rolled her eyes. "She's freaking obsessed with him. She probably thinks if she goes missing, Rich'll get all worried and freaked out and get back together with her. Well, that's never going to happen."

"Why not?" Winter had a feeling she knew where this was going.

Missy pressed her lips together. She might as well have zipped them, padlocked them, and tossed the key.

Winter fixed a hard gaze on the two women. "I hope both of you understand how serious this is. Nobody has seen or heard from Willa in months. Not her mom. Not her employer. An official missing persons investigation is underway—"

"Finally." Chelsea gave an exaggerated sigh.

"What do you mean?"

"I called the cops and told them all about this. About the fight, Rich dumping Willa for Missy, Willa catching Missy and Rich mashing." Chelsea waved her hand in the air. "I even reported Missy's missing dress because it's her favorite, it's seriously amazing on her, and they didn't do anything."

Winter could only imagine how that conversation went. *"Hi, I'm calling to file a missing persons and a missing formfitting-dress report."*

Between the two of them, Missy was seething from Chelsea's information dump, so Winter focused on her. "If you know anything that can help us understand where she might've gone or where she might be, it's very important that you speak up."

Missy jutted her chin up proudly. "I don't care."

"She could be in serious danger."

"She deserves whatever she gets."

"Not anything, Missy." Now that she'd decided to snitch,

Chelsea sounded more confident. "They were a terrible couple, you guys are much better, but we don't want her… you know."

The sensitive young woman couldn't even say the word *dead*. But Winter always appreciated people like Chelsea. The world would be a better place with more blurters in it.

Missy shot her roommate a death stare.

Winter forged ahead. "Tell me exactly what happened the last night you saw her."

"Why does it matter?" Missy clenched her fists.

"Willa was supposed to be going out with a bunch of her friends from high school." Chelsea was on a roll. "But, like, one of them had COVID or whatever, so they canceled. She came home way early and caught Missy and Rich making out on the couch."

"Okay. Fine." Missy huffed and planted her hands on her hips. "So what, huh? So Rich was sick and tired of her crap. So he didn't want to be with her anymore. He tried to tell her, but she wouldn't listen."

"So Willa comes in, sees you two together. What did she do?"

A self-satisfied smirk curled onto Missy's lips. "She freaked out. She screamed. Her and Rich argued a bunch. Then she packed her shit, *and my shit*, and left."

"Are you and Rich still together?"

"Yes. And I'm not sorry. I didn't do anything to Willa and neither did Rich." Missy sat on the bench next to the front door and pulled on some big black work shoes. "I'm done with this. I have to go to work now."

"One more question." Winter blocked her exit. "Where were you the rest of that night?"

Missy snatched up her purse and faced off with Winter. "Home with Chelsea." Then she slipped around Winter and was gone.

Winter turned back to Chelsea.

Her eyes were wide, head dipped to one side. "Do you really think Willa's hurt?"

"I'm afraid I can't answer that." The sinking feeling in her gut had an answer, but it wasn't the one anybody who cared about Willa wanted to hear. "Do you have Rich's contact information?"

Chelsea nodded and went to find her phone, while Winter tapped her foot and wondered how finding Willa York would lead her to Noah.

15

Winter stepped back into the hall, keying the address Chelsea had given her for Rich Benderell's workplace, Pinsky's Auto Repair, into her GPS. Chelsea said he wasn't always the best about answering his phone but that he'd be at work this time of day. It would be a seventeen-minute drive.

The door across the hall opened, and a man stepped out of apartment 406. He was tall and gangly with an oversize Adam's apple and limp, yellowy hair, maybe mid-thirties. A tied-up plastic bag sat on his welcome mat—a no-contact delivery that filled the hallway with the greasy smell of fried chicken. The man's eyes met hers, so Winter gave the obligatory polite nod and started to walk away.

"Excuse me?" The man stepped after her, his hand lifting as if reaching for her.

Winter paused and scanned his white polo shirt, tan pants, and wide ears. "Yes?"

"I was sitting in my living room when I overheard you talking to Chelsea. Are you here about Willa?"

A sharp chill licked down her back, forcing her to straighten. "And you are…?"

"Thatcher Templeton." He offered his hand. "I was here the night Willa left. After that big blowout."

"Did you know Willa well?"

He flattened his chin and shook his head. "Not too well. We'd chat when we passed in the hall sometimes. She was a really nice girl. After she left, I tried to talk to her roommates about it, but neither of them seemed to care. Actually, Missy would get really angry when I asked about her."

The chill spread to Winter's neck. "Are you saying you suspected something?"

Thatcher nodded, looking serious and thoughtful. "Her mother came by, and I even tried to speak to her about it, but she brushed me off too. I swear, it feels like I'm the only person who actually cares."

Winter could've told him that Nancy York came to her office looking for her daughter and went to the police, but she was far more interested in hearing what he had to say.

"I had a daughter, and I tell you, I would've moved heaven and earth to keep her safe. To find her if she went missing."

The change in his tone was sudden. One moment, he sounded like any friendly neighbor making conversation, and the next, he was gray and twitching with anger.

Winter picked up on the past tense. "I'm very sorry for your loss."

His gaze snapped to hers, and she swore she saw tears wobbling at the edges of his eyes. "It was a car accident."

"I'm sorry."

Looking at his shoes, Thatcher nodded a few times. When he lifted his head again, his voice was back to normal—the way it had been before he brought up his lost child. "I wanted to tell you that I saw Rich here the night Willa left."

"In the living room with Missy?"

"No. After. After Willa came back and caught him with

Missy, Rich stormed out before Willa did. I was relieved, because I was worried I was gonna have to call the cops for a domestic disturbance, but then I realized I never heard his bike firing up." He nodded toward the front side of the building. "I glanced out the window, and I saw him outside in the parking lot, pacing. Like he was waiting for Willa to come down."

Winter put her finger in her mouth to chew a nail, thought better of it, and forced her hand to her side. Time was short, so she decided to take a wild stab in the dark. "Does the name Erik Saulson mean anything to you?"

Thatcher Templeton furrowed his brow. "Is that another of their friends?"

She shook her head. The man seemed very interested in the lives of the girls across the hall. It was possible he was just a neighborhood busybody. Maybe he really did see Rich waiting for Willa. Or maybe he, like many a guilty man before him, was making the mistake of shoving himself into an investigation in an ill-advised attempt to endear himself to her and cast suspicion elsewhere.

"Do you make a habit of eavesdropping on your neighbors?"

Thatcher jerked his chin up. "As if I have a choice, when they're yelling at the top of their lungs. The walls in this building are paper-thin."

"Yelling about what?"

"About what a slut Missy is, about how she's selfish and only loves herself, about all Willa's done for Rich, about what a psycho Willa is, and how no one can stand her. Nasty girl stuff."

Winter glanced back at the trio's apartment door. "Did anybody threaten anyone? Get physical?"

"Only to never speak to each other again. I might've heard something hit the wall, or kick the wall. Might've been nothing. No one cried out in pain. Though Willa was crying pretty hard in general."

Winter took a step toward the elevator. It didn't appear Thatcher Templeton had any more useful information for her. She gave him a polite final smile. "Thank you for your help, Mr. Templeton."

❄

Pinsky's Auto Repair did a bit of everything but seemed to specialize in motorcycles. Winter found Rich Benderell sitting on his butt on the concrete next to a Kawasaki Ninja, poking at the engine with a long wrench.

The moment she saw him, she knew why Willa and Missy were fighting over him. The tousled locks, chiseled jaw, muscular shoulders—the grease monkey was all kinds of hot. The kind of guy she imagined smelled of equal parts engine oil and Ralph Lauren. The kind of guy who could get away with pretty much anything with one sloppy, uneven grin.

When Winter got his attention and told him Willa was missing, he looked genuinely shocked, perhaps even frightened. Or maybe he was nervous.

He wiped his hands on a rough yellow rag and sat back to peer up at her from where he sat on the ground, one wrist poised on his knee. "I didn't know. I swear."

His immediate defensiveness was one of the oldest and reddest flags in the book. That, plus the fear lurking in his eyes, suggested he did know something—something to do with Willa York. It didn't necessarily implicate him in her disappearance, but it sure as hell didn't exonerate him.

"When was the last time you saw her?"

He narrowed his eyes, staring vaguely at her knee. "I haven't seen or heard from Willa since that night…of our fight. Months ago."

The sounds of the garage echoed around them—more mechanics working a few bays down. It was hard to hear him, so she crouched. "What night?"

"The night we broke up."

"Would you mind walking me through it?"

Rich wiped sweat from his forehead with that same rough rag, leaving a smear of oil. The door from the office to the shop burst open, and a man dressed just like him walked in carrying a bunch of fast-food bags in one hand and a cup holder of sodas in the other.

Winter stood back up.

The man stopped near Rich, scanning Winter up and down as he held out a bag.

"Finally." Rich stood and took the bag without looking at him and set it aside.

The homey smell of fried chicken tickled Winter's nostrils for the second time that afternoon.

"Who's your friend?" the guy asked, giving Winter an approving side-eye.

"No one." Rich's face remained pale and pinched.

The other guy took the hint and wandered off to deliver the rest of the food to his coworkers.

"Please go on," Winter said.

Rich looked away. One of his legs twitched nervously. "Willa and me had been falling apart for a while. We both realized it needed to be over."

"So it was mutual?"

His eyes darted, refusing to meet hers, though she never once looked away.

He nodded.

"Okay." Winter chose not to contradict him just yet. She wanted to find out just how deep he was about to dig himself under. "How long were you together?"

"We met in high school, so, like, nine years. Maybe ten?"

"That's a long time."

"It wasn't that whole time. We've been on again, off again. We'd date for like six months, then break up, then get back together. It was a really toxic relationship." He pushed a lock of hair out of his eyes. "I'm sad she's missing, but I'm still glad it's over."

"How was it toxic?"

"Well…" He scratched the back of his neck with grease-stained fingernails. "Willa was really possessive and jealous. So freaking jealous. I swear, if I slept with half the people she accused me of…"

He took his phone out of his pocket and fiddled with the volume control, the screen flicking on and off with every touch. He was nervous, growing more so with every question. Good time to ask more.

"Who was she jealous of?"

"Everybody. Seriously. Willa would get so mad when I went out with my guy friends. She even got jealous when I was nice to her friends. It was ridiculous."

Well, you did end up sleeping with one of her friends.

"She never trusted me. She manipulated me. Threatened me." He looked down at the floor.

"What did she threaten you about?"

"Nothing," he snapped, a little too quickly.

"You just said she threatened you."

Rich raked his hands through his hair. His eyes had grown misty, like he was about to cry. "She always wanted to talk about our relationship and communication, and how we needed to make sacrifices to be together, but it was only ever things I needed to do. Things I needed to change. Like she was…"

Winter let him trail off and waited to see if he'd finish his sentence. She was very interested to hear the end of it.

"Never mind," he said.

"There sure are a lot of 'nothings' and 'never minds' in this conversation." She searched his face for a moment. "So what happened the night you broke up? Where did it all go down?"

"Her place. We got together and talked and decided it was time to end it. She gave me my stuff, and I left."

"So that was the last time you saw her?"

"Yes. It was a couple days before she moved out."

He was lying. Maybe he was covering his ass, thinking the cops would home in on him, since he was the ex-boyfriend of a missing woman. He wouldn't be wrong about that. There was a damn good reason investigators always looked at close relations first.

Statistics suggested he was probably guilty. She had the sense he wasn't going to own up to the truth unless she slapped him in the face with it, and she didn't have time to do it any other way.

"Okay." Winter scribbled on the edge of the notebook. "So is that the same night Willa found out you and Missy were having an affair?"

Rich's face, if anything, paled further, and his lips parted. Belatedly, he made a concerted effort to recover with a weak, incredulous chuckle. "What?"

Winter looked right into his eyes. He still refused to meet hers even for a second.

"Before you answer, I spoke to Missy Stoder and Chelsea Gray. They told me what happened, and others in the building confirmed it. So I guess my next question would be, why is your story different from everyone else's?"

He took a step back. "Missy told you about us?"

"Mm-hmm. She seemed kind of proud."

"Dammit. Fine." He raked his hands through his messy hair again, making it even messier. "I was screwing Missy behind Willa's back. But it's not what you think."

"What do I think?"

"I didn't have anything to do with it."

"To do with what?"

He growled in frustration. "With whatever happened to Willa."

"What happened to Willa?"

"I mean her leaving or being missing right now." Rich lifted an oily finger and shook it in her face. "Dammit. You're not gonna trick me into making myself look bad. I don't have to talk to you without a lawyer."

You are perfectly capable of looking bad all on your own.

"I'm not a cop. I'm just someone who's trying to find Willa." Winter lifted her shoulders. "You don't have to talk to me at all, but if you want Willa to be found…and if you don't have anything to hide, I don't see any reason why you wouldn't."

"I didn't do anything." He threw the rag to the ground, cheeks pinking as his breath quickened. "We were over. For good this time. I'm with Missy now. I love Missy. I don't owe Willa anything. I can't live my whole life—"

Rich cut himself off, looking sad and broken.

Winter sensed a secret at the tip of his tongue, but then he swallowed it, and his face hardened. Whatever he'd almost been ready to tell her, he'd changed his mind and buried it deeper than ever before.

He said he didn't owe her anything, which meant he probably *did* owe her something. But what?

"If you know something that might help us find Willa, and you don't tell us, that would really make you look bad."

His eyes hardened, and he shook his head. "I hope you find her. I really, really do. I would never want anything bad to happen to her. But I haven't seen her since that night. She blocked me across all platforms within hours of leaving her apartment. This was pretty typical of her too. I just…I just thought maybe our breakup finally stuck. Like I said, it was a long time coming, and I don't know anything. I swear."

"Okay. Thank you for your time." Winter turned on her heel and took a step away, knowing full well she wasn't ready to leave just yet. She closed her eyes and took a deep breath through her nose. Ralph Lauren and motor oil. "By the way, a neighbor said that after the yelling stopped, they saw you pacing in the parking lot. They thought you looked like you were waiting for someone."

She watched him in the shine of chrome, upside down and distorted. He rubbed the back of his neck and swayed nervously on shuffling feet.

"I felt too wound up to ride. I was just smoking a cigarette to try to cool down before getting on my bike. Isn't that what I'm supposed to do?"

"Atta boy." Winter shot him a smile. "My next question, of course, is where did you go when you eventually left?"

"Home."

"Alone?"

He nodded gruffly. "Why is that any of your business?"

"I guess that means nobody can vouch for where you were?"

His fists tightened, all the nervousness crystalizing into rage. "Yes, I was alone, but I didn't do anything to hurt Willa. I would never hurt her, no matter what. You gotta believe me."

"Sure. Why wouldn't I? I mean, you've been so forthcoming so far." Winter looked him up and down, at last catching his eyes. Then she smiled coldly and left without another word.

16

Before heading to her grandparents' house for dinner, Winter drove through the darkening roads in her own neighborhood. She looked for signs of Noah in the bushes, trees, and ditches. She drove past her house to see if anything new had been taped to the door.

Nothing but shadows. Her house looked lonely. The flowers in the pots on the front porch had begun to droop. She thought back to the day Noah planted them—outside in cargo shorts, flip-flops, and a big, floppy hat. She'd called him a dork, and he'd sprayed her with the hose.

A laugh formed like a bubble in her throat but escaped her lips as a sob. Soft trembles overcame her shoulders. She curled into herself, hands wrenching like claws near her chest. Her breath caught in her lungs, and when she finally let it out, with it came the tears. Digging into Willa's disappearance hadn't gotten her any closer to finding Noah. Not yet anyway. And she was vibrating with fear over what was happening to him.

She cried uncontrollably for about thirty seconds, then got ahold of herself, reeled it in, and forced it back down.

Donning sunglasses to cover her swollen eyes, she got out and watered the flowers. Noah would be upset if all his plants were dead when he came home. She needed to keep everything nice for him.

Thinking of this, she went inside and watered the ficus and monstera and moved the dirty dishes from the sink into the dishwasher. She turned off the coffeepot, which she'd left on warm for the last two days. Coffee was caked inside the carafe, dried on like superglue. She filled it with soapy water, left it to soak, and stared out the window over the sink.

Where was he? She kept trying to link the events. Cybil stepped in just after Willa went missing. That had to be intentional, orchestrated by Erik Saulson. But what had Willa York done to warrant her possible kidnapping and murder?

She had to face the fact that people who disappeared for three months didn't generally reappear. So Erik found Cybil in a community of haters and planted her at Poole's so she could destroy the psychologist for ruining her childhood by having an affair with her dad. He then used Cybil as a means to get messages to Winter.

Now Erik had taken Noah and seemed to be using Willa's disappearance to get more cryptic messages to her. Unfortunately, none of it told her where Noah was or explained Erik's interest in York.

Was York simply in the wrong place at the wrong time? Winter did not buy that.

She went up to their room and picked out an outfit for tomorrow. No more than that. By tomorrow night, she'd be back in her own house, sleeping in her own bed, with Noah next to her.

❄

At dinner that night, Winter learned her grandmother had the same innate urge to feed her that Eve had. Gramma Beth had made a dinner of roast chicken, mashed potatoes, rosemary gravy, and pan-fried collard greens, with triple fudge brownies for dessert. Winter ate a large helping of everything and two brownies, along with some of her feelings. Why not? They tasted like chocolate.

Later, alone in her twin-size bed, Winter fought with herself about whether to call Noah's mom and tell her what had happened. Noah had been missing for going on two days now. She wasn't trying to keep that information hidden from anyone. At the same time, she didn't want to worry his mom unnecessarily. And if she found out Noah was missing, she'd come to Austin. There'd be no stopping her.

Winter put down her phone and flicked off the light. One more day. That was all she needed. She'd find Noah and bring him home safe. There was no reason to worry her. Not yet.

Grampa Jack had offered her another sleeping pill, which apparently was some kind of highly addictive opiate. She'd taken it that first night without question, but now that she knew what it was, it sat beside her water bottle on the nightstand. She couldn't risk anything clouding her wits.

That left Winter lying awake in bed with her mind racing a million miles a minute. She was half tempted to call Eve. She'd offered to be her surrogate Noah, after all. If he were there in bed beside her and she was feeling like this, she'd have woken him up and made him talk to her about it.

She didn't want to bother Eve, though. The woman had already put herself on 24-7 patrol, in addition to everything she was doing to work on the case. Winter didn't want to bug her with her dang emotional issues too.

Rising from bed, she headed downstairs for a glass of milk and maybe another brownie. She'd reached the landing in the middle of the stairwell when a sharp stabbing pain drilled into the side of her head and drove her to her knees. She clapped her hands over her ears, trying to shut out the bright shrieking that shot through her mind. Blood on her lips, streaming from her nose. Everything drew in so tight, she forgot to breathe. All at once, she fell into the vision.

Skeletal limbs of trees tangled above her, just like before. Only there was something different about them now. The tree was thorny and bleeding, dripping down to spatter her face.

"Winter!"

"Noah?" She scrambled to her feet, even as the prickly, low-hanging branches tore at her flesh. The thorns were swelling like ticks filling with blood. Slowly, they took on the appearance of tiny fingers.

Disgusted, she recoiled. The fingers grew and grew until they were human sized. Then, one by one, they exploded and bloomed. Each finger became a red dahlia. The flowers were as perfect as if they were made of glass. Trails of blood swam among the geometric petals.

A dog barked—small and distant. She whirled around and watched as a gray-and-white Jack Russell retreated down a path through dozens of trees. She jogged after it, following a circuitous path. The wind kicked up, sending a rain of red petals swirling like snowflakes in a blizzard.

"Winter," Noah called again, softer and closer than before. As the dog rounded a bend in the trees, Noah came into view in his jogging shorts and bare feet. The dog ran to his side and began to hop up and down at his shins.

"Noah!" She tried to run for him, but her foot found no purchase, and she plunged into a pit of wet red dahlias.

Winter screamed, but no noise came out.

Carpet fibers scratched at her cheek, and Winter shot bolt upright on the landing of the stairs. Trembling, she drew her knees to her chest and wiped her nose on the back of her hand. A small red puddle stained the gray carpet.

The sound of Grampa Jack sawing logs in the bedroom helped to ground her in reality, away from the dream of the finger trees and the dahlias. She wanted to cry, but it was like her eyes were empty.

Everything was empty. Noah was gone, and without him, she was just a shell of the person she was supposed to be. Agonizing loneliness wrapped around her like a soggy blanket. She missed him so much, his absence was like enduring the phantom pains of an amputated limb. Or so she imagined.

The ache of longing spread out to her family in Richmond—for her best friend, Autumn Trent, and all the agents at the FBI office there who'd meant so much to her. The people she had always trusted to carry her through any crisis.

Her grandparents were here, and she could lean on them, but they couldn't help her fight the monsters that refused to leave her alone. If anything, her love for them only made her more vulnerable.

Dizzy and shaking, Winter coaxed herself back up to her room. She fell on the bed, snatched her phone in her numb fingers, and called the only number she had left to call.

It rang only twice before she got an answer.

"Winter? Are you okay?" Eve's voice was groggy and thin. Clearly, she'd just roused from sleep.

Winter glanced at the clock on the wall. It was past three in morning.

"I'm okay. I'm..." Her voice cracked on the lie. She balled a fist and pressed it into her knee. "I'm not okay."

"I'm on my way."

17

Winter rested her forehead against her fingers and looked out the window of the SUV at the retreating darkness. Eve was in the driver's seat, both hands on the wheel as they slowly crept through the neighborhood near Winter and Noah's house—looking, once again, at all the places he might've been last and seeing nothing.

For most of her life, Winter had kept her visions a secret from pretty much everybody. Given the field she worked in, most of her colleagues were pragmatic people who did not want to entertain the possibility of the existence of anything remotely supernatural.

Winter would've agreed with that viewpoint if the validity of her visions hadn't been proven time and time again. She couldn't possibly count the number of cases wherein they'd helped her find hidden clues and solve crimes that otherwise seemed impossible.

When her visions became pertinent to a case, she often concocted reasons why she seemed to know things that technically she should not. Tonight, however, Winter didn't have the energy. She needed someone to help her sort through what she'd seen. Twice now.

She was too close to the situation—flustered and confused. Sometimes, simply explaining her dreams out loud was enough to help her understand their purpose. Other times, all she needed was for somebody else to ask her questions, and it would all snap together.

Her best friend was the perfect person to do that, but Autumn had her own troubles right now, and Winter couldn't bring herself to heap hers on top of them.

But anything that might help her find Noah was worth the risk, even if it meant Eve Taggart thought she was a grade A quack.

After Winter finished explaining about her dreams, Eve stayed quiet, squinting at the road and sipping from her metal coffee mug. She'd turned up at Winter's grandparents' house less than twenty minutes after receiving the call, so she'd clearly dressed in the dark.

The blue windbreaker was way too big for her—her husband's, perhaps. Her long, pale-blond hair was wrapped up in a messy bun on top of her head, and her makeup-free face looked pale and puffy from sleep.

"Okay." Eve dropped her mug into the cup holder and gripped the wheel with both hands. "I'm sorry about your brain."

Winter pulled her lips tight. She hadn't said much about why she got visions, only that she suffered a head injury as a child that required surgery, and then she woke up with the ability and obligation to see things others could not. She kept to herself the violent circumstances surrounding that energy, though there was a chance Eve already knew about them. So much of Winter's life was a matter of public record, and FBI agents were by and large curious types.

"So you think these things mean something? The flowers and the trees and the dog and all that?"

"Yes, they mean something." They pulled up to a stop sign in the empty residential street. Winter watched a squirrel run across a telephone wire on the other side of the intersection. "I know you must think I'm insane."

"Doesn't matter what I think. And for the record, I don't think you're insane. My grandfather always used to say, *'Conosco i miei polli. E le volpi?'*"

"What?"

"I know my chickens, but what about the foxes? It's a reminder that you can easily miss what happens even in your own backyard. So always keep your eyes and your mind open."

Winter attempted a smile and peered back out the window.

"So obviously, we got Noah in his shorts out for jog, right? Did it seem like the dog was his?"

"No. He never looked at it."

"Okay. And he wasn't wearing any shoes—"

She shook her head. "He was trying to get me to follow him."

"Right. Leading you to him, showing you where he is. It has to be the dog, right?"

Winter nibbled on her fingertip. "Have you seen any Jack Russells around here?"

"Maybe. If only we could narrow down his route."

"You said you saw him in the CCTV?"

"Yeah, mostly right by your house. He was headed vaguely southwest. But he was just out for a jog, so he wasn't actually going anywhere."

She slumped in her seat. "Maybe we could contact the HOAs around here. They might keep track of who owns dogs and what breed."

"It's far more useful to assume he was going somewhere." Eve drummed her fingers on the steering wheel in quick succession, her energy waxing as morning twilight broke on the horizon. "If Noah were jogging to an actual place, where would he be going?"

"But he wasn't going anywhere."

"Hey, if I go along with blizzards of blood dahlias and prophetic terriers, the least you can do is come along on my little thought experiments, m'kay?"

Winter snorted in spite of herself. A little knot she'd been carrying in her lungs since she woke up on the stairs came undone. She inhaled deeply. "I dunno. Probably going back to the hardware store."

"Why?"

"That's the nature of hardware stores, isn't it? He'd just come from there, so the chances he forgot something or got something wrong are about fifty-fifty." Her head fell gently against her hand, thinking of him. "Every time he did anything in the garden or for the house, he bitched about it. *'Decorated intelligence agent but can't figure out how to buy the right size damn screws. I'm going back to the hardware store.'*"

"Nice Noah impression. Which one? Which way is it?"

Straightening in her seat, Winter lifted a finger to point. She said the words out loud as they hit her. "Vaguely southwest."

Eve guided the SUV along the route. As they crawled along, Winter scanned the yards—looking for fences, signs of digging, or yellow patches in the grass. Or wandering Jack Russells.

As they passed by the lot of an elementary school, something red caught Winter's eye. "Pull over."

Eve swerved and parked.

A chain-link fence encircled a large soccer field. Tied to the chain at even intervals were hundreds of tiny red ribbons. A brisk wind combed through them, causing them to shift and swirl like petals.

"What is it?" Eve leaned in close, her gaze following Winter's toward the fence.

"I want to get out here." Popping the SUV door, Winter stepped out into the cool morning.

Eve was close behind her.

Their boots on the concrete were the only sound as they approached the fence. Winter ran her fingertips over the plastic ribbons. "I've never been here before."

Eve touched her back lightly and took a step away. She shoved her hands in her pockets and paced down the street. Winter went the other direction. The houses in this neighborhood had a lot of space between them, trees and rhododendrons growing in between. A streetlamp winked on a green road sign half hidden in the branches. *Dahlia Lane.*

Winter's heartbeat quickened. "Eve?"

She was a few houses down, shining her flashlight at a puddle. She jogged to Winter's side. "What's up?"

"Dahlia." She pointed to the street sign.

Eve swept her flashlight to it synchronously with her eyes. "Huh."

"We're close. It has to be on this street. Somewhere."

Side by side, they moved down the dusty road. Somewhere in an alleyway, a garbage truck was working, the sky growing pale purple in the early light.

They walked a few blocks down Dahlia Lane, past a small goat farm and several huge hedges of rhododendrons. Winter kept hoping she'd see something glowing red—a fresh signal from her brain that she was close.

Nothing. They might have to walk the same route several times, but she wasn't about to give up. Her visions, while painful and confusing, always led her to something. One way or the other.

A low growl caught her ear. As they moved past an untrimmed patch of trees at the corner of an intersection, Winter twitched to attention and rushed into the brush.

Wiry brown fur moved through the foliage.

"Here, dog. Come here."

She ducked under a heavy limb and stepped into a puddle of gloppy mud. The dog barked and growled, hopping up and down on his little paws. A whiskered smile said he was not aggressive, just playful. He was a Jack Russell all right, but so covered in mud, it would've been impossible to say what color his fur was supposed to be.

"It's okay. I won't hurt you." As she held her hand out to the dog to let him sniff her, a flicker of metal caught her eye. She wiped her thumb over the tag on his collar and read *Milo*.

"Who's a good boy, Milo?" She patted his disgusting head, getting more mud on her palm. He turned his back on her and returned to what he he'd been doing—gnawing on an object under a bush. "What you got there?"

Something bright green shined under a pile of mud. She caught hold of it and lifted up Noah's size fourteen running shoe.

Everything hit Winter at once, as if the clouds above broke open and soaked her in freezing rain. In her mind's eye, she could see what had happened. Noah coming around this corner, not knowing what was waiting for him. Something hitting him so hard it literally knocked his shoe off.

She raked her fingers through her hair, her breaths growing faster, closer together. Red clouded her eyes as if with an oncoming vision, a metallic taste coating her throat. But no vision came. When she opened her mouth to call Eve over, all that came out was a scream.

18

Eve called an FBI team out to canvass the scene and to enter the shoe into evidence. They only found the one shoe—covered in dog saliva and mud, chewed into submission. The chances they'd find any useful physical evidence on it were virtually nil.

And it was impossible not to have the FBI and police out in the open now, no matter how much Winter wanted to play by Erik Saulson's rules.

All the same, as the sun rose over Dahlia Lane, it was clear an auto accident had taken place near the site of the missing shoe. No cameras were pointed at the blind corner, but the skid marks on the asphalt looked fresh. From what Eve could see, a vehicle had accelerated into the turn and then stopped short.

Initial interviews with residents uncovered no witnesses. But one woman who lived closer to the school confirmed seeing Noah jog past her house just before lunchtime.

With that testimony, Eve could nail down the time of the abduction to between eleven thirty and noon. There were no sidewalks in this area, so Noah would've been running on the shoulder. As he rounded the corner, the driver of the vehicle accelerated and struck him. His shoe came off in the impact.

Noah had not been the victim of a simple hit-and-run. Otherwise, they would've located him in any of Austin's many hospitals. Winter had dutifully called them all the night he went missing. He would've been wearing his military dog tags. He always wore them. Besides, he was six-four and built like a dump truck. The man was hardly inconspicuous.

After striking Noah, it seemed the driver of the vehicle had gathered him up and driven away with him. If they could find the car that left those skid marks, they'd find Noah. But where to start? Maybe Winter could conjure up another vision. It seemed to be working just fine so far.

Eve felt a headache coming on. Things were starting to get weird, though it could've just been that she'd only slept a few hours in the last two days. Jackie's cold had turned out to be the flu, so the second she walked in the door, she was on mommy duty for both her children and her husband until she had to leave again.

The poor man was trying. He wasn't one of those man-babies who fell apart the second he got a sniffle. Her husband would fight through to the end and make himself sicker and sicker. She had to mommy him by making him take his medicine, get in a bath, and then go to bed.

She hoped he'd been okay this morning—alone, sick as death, getting their psycho broodlings off to school on time.

Worrying about her husband was just another thumbtack in her guts. Eve felt like she'd swallowed a whole case of them when she looked at Winter and saw the gray worry streaked across her face.

Hugging her arms to her chest, she walked to the edge of the yellow tape where Winter stood. Her gaze was elsewhere, as her mind often seemed to be.

If her visions were real—and there was no reason to think they weren't, other than it was kind of insane—then it actually explained a lot.

As partners, Noah and Eve had talked a lot on long drives and boring office days together. His favorite subject of conversation was Winter. She was also the source of most of the stress in his life. Every move he made was always in consideration of her—to help her, be near her, protect her—while she remained as passionate and unpredictable as fire.

"We're going over every inch of the area," Eve said. "If there's anything to find here, we will find it."

Winter nibbled on the tip of her thumb and index finger. "I know."

"You should go try to get some rest. You look like death."

She nodded, her eyes landing on the bush where they'd found Noah's shoe. "Did you find Milo's owners?"

"Yeah. He's fine. Winter?"

"Yeah?"

"You need to sleep."

"I will."

"Don't bullshit me." Eve covered her face with both her hands and heaved a groan. "I'm going to take you back to your grandma's house, and you're going to sleep."

"Do you think there's any video games about dahlias or bleeding trees?"

"What?"

"Saulson and all the *Final Fantasy* stuff. Do you think maybe in my dream there could be some kind of gamer code that I don't understand?"

This line of questioning was getting a little too weird even for Eve. "Um. I think I don't know anything about psychics or video games, so—"

"I've been standing here trying to look up gamer stuff on my phone." Winter's voice was high and reedy, her body jerky. It seemed she'd gone right past sleepy into a new level of tired. "My eyes just glaze over. I might as well be trying to learn Russian. There're board games, video games, game developers, game design, fan fiction...it's too much. Unless I could find out exactly which media Saulson's been consuming, there's no way to use it to know what game he's playing. What the damn rules are. What I'm supposed to do to win."

Eve gently guided Winter toward her vehicle. "Come on. Let's get in the car."

"Saulson wants me to find Willa York, so that's exactly what I'm going to do. If I do what he wants, it'll lead to Noah, and he'll have to let him go, right?"

Eve didn't answer, and it was clear from the pain in Winter's eyes that she didn't need to. The chances that Erik Saulson would honor his word were negligible. Maybe there was no choice but to go along with his game, but there were also no guarantees. Saulson was the sort of person who'd kill his own partner, so it was highly likely he didn't have any qualms about lying to his victims.

19

"I see you, Erik." Hitting the Print button, I leaned back from my keyboard with a satisfied smirk. Not only had I found the son of a bitch's real name, but now I knew where he worked. I knew who his dad was. In fact, I had everything I needed to destroy him if he failed to deliver on his promise.

Gotta love a narcissist's confidence. He was certain he was so much smarter than everyone around him, including me. Maybe especially me. He thought I was delusional and weak, and maybe I was. But I wasn't a moron.

I wondered if Winter Black had figured out his real name too.

If so, that wouldn't be good for us.

With a heavy belch, I rose from my squeaky chair and staggered to the kitchen. I'd already eaten dinner, but screw it. I snatched another meal from the freezer and tossed it in the microwave. I couldn't stop thinking about Winter Black or Noah.

Erik had succeeded in finding the one thing that could break her, and he used me to accomplish his goal. But to what end?

Wandering back to my desk—an old card table held steady with cinder blocks—I snatched up the thick pile of papers on my printer.

I had no plausible deniability. I knew I was culpable in everything he'd done.

"His finger. I cut off his finger…" The words hurt my throat, but when I tried to think back on what I'd done, it all seemed blurry. Just like with Willa, it was like it had happened to someone else.

People who claimed to have blacked out while doing horrible things always seemed full of shit to me. Now I had to concede their point.

I'd done my part and handed in my "payment" to get the final bit of information I needed. I left the package in the spot Erik told me to, and he promised that when he picked it up, he'd send me the name of the driver. Along with some video.

I checked the phone again—the one only Erik used. No new messages.

"Be patient." I riffled through the papers while I waited for the microwave to ding. "Erik would have to be insane to screw me over on this. He ought to know I meant it when I said I would break all his bones. Or maybe…the bolt cutters." Laughter bubbled in my throat, thinking of Erik screaming and bleeding on the floor in front of me.

Winter Black. Why else would she be looking for Willa… unless Erik set her on the scent somehow?

Erik was threatening to expose me. But he didn't know I was not a damn mouse. I was a honey badger, and I'd rip his face off. Maybe Erik would learn that lesson soon.

The microwave beeped. I slapped down the stack of papers on the desk and started toward it when the phone finally buzzed.

A text message. A name and an address...and the rest of the video.

The stupid bastard told me himself. I can prove it.

I clicked open the attachment and turned up the volume. This burner phone was garbage, so I didn't know if the video was poor quality or just the screen. Still, there were his words, clear as a bell. And there was his face. The man in the footage was very drunk. Young. Blond hair. Crying and confessing his part in the accident. He was a sloppy fucking mess.

He said Willa's name more than once. *"Little girl,"* he said, and *"died almost immediately."*

How he ran away.

Why he ran away.

Thinking only of himself and leaving Quincy—my daughter—to die.

Game on! Erik texted.

For once, I had to agree with the little freak.

20

Rich Benderell knew from experience that throwing himself into taxing work was the best way to get out of his own brain. So when closing time at the auto shop rolled around, he volunteered to stay and lock up so he could finish installing the transmission replacement he'd been working on all day. He slid under the compact sedan and held the transmission in place with his legs while he tightened the bolts.

Rich's legs wavered under the strain, burning and trembling with each crank of the wrench. The shop kept a lift for such things, of course, but he craved the physical exhaustion.

With the transmission installed, he headed to the sales floor to straighten and restock all the shelves for morning. He absentmindedly organized the shelf of engine oils and other fluids, not even seeing the names or price tags as he worked, just ensuring each product stood at the front of its designated shelf.

His mind wandered as he worked, roaming the store like a car without a driver. Finally, he made his way to the cashier's desk and sorted the air fresheners in the rotating display there.

Rich not only didn't want to go home, he wanted to pretend his home didn't exist. Missy had been texting him all afternoon and evening, trying to get him to call, to come over.

At first, she'd been trying to reason with him. *We need to talk about this. We need to make sure we're on the same page.* Then she tried to commiserate. *I know how hard this is on you, baby, but I'm not going to let Willa tear us apart. Alive or dead.*

Rich cringed at that before shoving it hard out of his brain. Missy thought she understood, but she didn't know the half of it.

He'd never told her the truth, and he never would. Finding out Willa was missing was bad enough before that nosy P.I. showed up and started asking too many questions. The moment she left, all the guys had been up in his business, and their pestering had continued into today. Rich volunteered to change the transmission mostly so he could hide under a car, put in his earbuds, and pretend he was somewhere else.

It hadn't worked. Every song on the shop's playlist reminded him of Willa, and every memory of Willa led him back to the worst night of his life. Over and over, he heard the sharp cries of the dying girl as if he were right back on the street corner—wailing with snot leaking down his face as he begged Willa to save him from the horrible mess he'd made…and himself.

Eight long years had passed since that night. He'd let it control him for so long. It was the only reason he'd stayed with Willa as long as he had. He'd fallen out of love with her years ago.

What he'd told Winter Black was true—his and Willa's

relationship had been nothing but ten different flavors of toxicity.

They'd meshed well in high school, when all he cared about was having a good time. That had all changed the night he got behind the wheel—drunk, tripping balls on shrooms, and not taking any of it seriously. Someone else had paid the price that night—an innocent little girl who never even got the chance to make half the stupid decisions he'd made during those hours.

Rich wasn't the same person after that. A piece of him had died on the road that night with that little girl.

He flicked off the computer and opened the till to count out the cash. He was so distracted that by the time he was done counting, he had no idea just how much he had.

With a heavy sigh, he slumped over the register. Every time he blinked, flashes of that night assaulted his senses like an oncoming seizure. He was nineteen. They were coming from a pregame party and on their way to a concert downtown put on by a local band one of his friends played in.

Heading to the car, he snatched her keys from her hand as he'd always done, and Willa questioned him. Asked him if he wanted her to drive. That was his clearest memory from that night. Maybe his only memory.

Willa was different back then—punk rock personified, with Vans on her feet and streaks of neon green in her hair. Rich hadn't listened to her question or thought about the danger. The lightheaded, giggly feeling of the mushrooms had started to rush over him, and he'd snatched Willa by the waist, kissing her so deep and stealing a little squeeze of her boobs.

Then he'd given her a spank and gotten behind the wheel.

It was just starting to get dark, streetlamps pulsing in his twisted vision. Rich had been teasing Willa about some dude who was hitting on her back at the party. He'd had one hand on the wheel, the other on his phone, flicking through texts. In his periphery, the pinprick freckles on Willa's cleavage were just beginning to dance.

They were so pretty. She was so pretty, or so he'd thought back when he still loved her.

Rich had thought he was Tokyo Drift back then. He liked the way Willa screamed and giggled when he took corners too fast and left black streaks on the asphalt. She liked to fall against him as if they were in their own private tilt-a-whirl. He gave her a giant, shit-eating grin as he went whipping around a blind corner too fast, waiting for her to shriek with delight.

He hadn't seen the yellow lights blinking to warn him to stop or the little girl walking her dog across the crosswalk.

Willa screamed first with joy and then in horror. He felt the bump—something slapping against the hood, then falling and being sucked under the wheels.

Blood spattered the windshield. For a moment, he was mesmerized by the blood and the way it dripped down the glass.

He thought he'd hit a big bird or a deer. He'd even laughed at Willa's dramatic response before he heard the heartbreaking scream of the little girl—who he learned later was only nine years old. She'd died moments after impact.

The street was empty. There were no witnesses, except the dog, who paced back and forth by his fallen human, barking incessantly.

The mushrooms hadn't fully kicked in until he was standing over the dead body. He thought he kept seeing the dead girl blink every time he looked away. Her skin was covered in paisley designs, and tiny red flowers he knew weren't really there dusted the concrete and asphalt all around. They bloomed and closed back up, over and over.

When he looked at his own hands, all he saw were grotesque, moss-covered claws. Then, when he looked back at the little girl, she sat up. All her broken bones popped and crackled, brains and blood dripping from the open wound in her skull.

He'd stood like a slack-jawed statue as Willa tried to revive the dead girl, and the dead girl laughed at her pathetic efforts. Willa started to cry, her face going as red and flat as a stop sign.

"She's dead!" Willa's voice had pierced his hallucination. *"We need to call 911!"*

At first, her words hadn't registered. When she pulled out her phone to call the cops, survival instinct suddenly kicked in. Without really thinking about it, Rich had slapped the phone out of her hand.

He'd been in trouble with the police ever since he'd discovered alcohol at fifteen. He already had seven underage drinking tickets. His license had been suspended. Willa didn't know about that because she wouldn't let him drive if she did. Standing on the street over the bleeding, broken body of the child he'd killed, the truth spilled out like projectile vomit.

If the cops found him like this, he'd go to prison. Not to jail for a month or two—but serious federal prison and for a very long time.

His life flashed before him, followed by all the life he was about to lose over one stupid mistake. Willa was all he had, his only hope. Rich fell to his knees, tears and snot streaking his face, and began to beg. At first, even he wasn't sure exactly what he wanted her to do.

"Please, you have to help me. Please." *He grabbed her hands and yanked them to his chest.*

She cried out, saying he was hurting her, and scrambled back away from him. Rich followed her, tearing up his knees as he shuffled across the pavement to snatch her fingers and press them to his chest.

"We have to call the cops." Willa shook her head, her eyes wide and round in disbelief. "If we just tell the truth—"

"No!" he screamed, more snot than syllable. "If you turn me in, I'll never see you again. They'll put me away forever."

"No, they won't. It was an accident. You—"

"I'm tripping balls!" He pressed the back of her hand to his cheek, refusing to let go. "You have to help me. Please, baby. Please. You have to, or you'll never see me again."

He'd never forget how horrified she'd looked in that moment. She couldn't believe what he was asking. "We can't just leave her."

"I have to. You don't understand." Rich stumbled to his feet and backed away. "Nobody can know the truth, you hear me? Nobody. You were alone. You got distracted. You hit her."

"Rich, don't ask me to do this. It's not fair. I can't...I don't think I can lie about something like this."

A sharp stab of fear and the all-consuming need to protect himself propelled him to take another step back and then another.

"You're sober. You have no priors, and you're a minor. If you say you did it, you'll get off. I know you will."

"Where are you going?" Tears sparkled like glitter in her eyes.

He remembered thinking they looked so pretty.

Before Willa could protest any further or try to reason with him, Rich had turned tail and run away from the scene. Back then, he was a horrible, selfish toad who only cared about his own freedom, his own survival.

To this day, he didn't really understand why Willa had gone along with it and taken the fall. Probably just so she could hold it over him for the rest of his life—which was exactly what had happened.

Now, eight years later—eight years sober from weed, Molly, psychedelics—all Rich felt when he thought about what he'd done was shame. He'd killed a little girl and then left his girlfriend to take the fall. Willa called 911 and confessed to everything. She was arrested and charged with involuntary manslaughter. The authorities called her witch of a mom to bail her out.

After the trial, Willa was given a fine, served six months out of two-year sentence, and was put on probation, but that was nothing compared to what they would've done to Rich. He could've served up to twenty years. With his record and given how recklessly irresponsible he'd been to get behind the wheel in his state, they'd have thrown the book at him.

Twenty years might as well have been a life sentence. There was no coming back from that, not really. Willa saved his life that night. He was tied to her with chains of guilt and duty. Willa had been there with him on the worst night of his entire life. She'd rescued him.

And she never let him forget that.

Every time they got close to breaking up, every time he wanted to do something that she didn't, every time he dared to disagree, Willa would bring up what she'd done for him.

Rich had traded twenty years in prison for a life sentence with a woman he didn't love.

Missy didn't know the truth, as much as he'd been tempted to tell her. And the more time he spent with Missy, the more she convinced him he'd paid his dues. She told him he didn't deserve to always be unhappy. Slowly, over a period of several months as he fell in love, he came to believe her.

He'd wanted so badly to tell Missy his secret, but the only person he'd ever told the truth to was a random stranger in a bar. They'd both been sitting there—minding their own business, drowning their sorrows in their drug of choice—when the guy had leaned in and said, *"You look like a guy with a sad story. Wanna trade?"*

Rich had laughed, but their conversation kept circling back to regrets. Back to sin. He got drunker and drunker.

The guy was a really passionate speaker. He'd gone off about relative morality, the constrictions of society, and toxic femininity.

"*Fear is the mother of morality,*" the stranger said, adding that it was a quote from some dude called Nietzsche. *"I can tell you feel guilty about something. Maybe if you said it out loud, it wouldn't have so much power over you."*

Rich broke down. For so long, he'd wanted just to tell somebody—anybody—what he'd done. He wanted to tell the truth to a human face and watch it twist with all the horror and revulsion he knew he deserved.

They'd left the bar and stumbled down the street together, sharing a bottle of gin, when Rich finally blurted it all out. He told the story of killing the girl in as much detail as he could remember—the bare truth as he understood it. With tears in his eyes, he even went so far as to admit he was cheating on his girlfriend because he didn't love her. He confessed he only stayed with her because he was afraid of what she might do to him, should he try to leave.

Rich had expected the stranger to be shook. To gasp or spit on him or call the police. He'd wanted him to. He hadn't wanted to live with the guilt anymore. But that wasn't what the stranger did at all.

"We all make mistakes, bro," the man had said, clapping a hand on his shoulder. *"We all have skeletons. You learned your lesson, right? Torturing yourself doesn't help anyone. 'Sides, the cops probably wouldn't listen to your girl even if she did come clean."*

Rich had swiped at the tears still falling from his eyes. *"Of course they'd listen to her. It's a felony offense!"*

"Don't be stupid. It's so easy. All you gotta do is catch her acting crazy and then deny everything. First things first, bro. Leave her ass. Drop her like a hot brick and make sure she's real mad about it. Don't try to keep her cool. Let that bitch act crazy. Pump her up

and make her go pop with the crazy. Then, if she goes to the cops, they'll know you just dumped her ass, and she's trying to get back on that D, bro."

For months after that night, he was paranoid that his whole life was about to come crashing down all around him at any moment. But it didn't. The stranger—they'd never exchanged names—had been true as his word. He'd listened to his confession and kept it to himself.

In an odd way, the interaction had helped restore his faith in humanity. And it gave him hope that he might be entitled to a little bit of happiness. Just a morsel.

Still, if Missy ever found out the truth, she'd never look at him the same. And the way she looked at him—like he was a good person and not one of the biggest pieces of shit to ever crawl out of a womb—had become his reason for living.

He wanted to be the person Missy believed he was.

He thought about the little girl a lot. Not a day went by that he didn't think of her mother and father and all the pain he'd put them through. The girl would've been about seventeen this year, nearly as old as he was when he killed her. She should be having her first kiss, going to prom, getting her driver's license.

Instead, she was rotting in a child-sized coffin in a dark corner of a graveyard.

Quincy. Her name was Quincy.

Tears spackled Rich's cheeks, which he wiped away on the sleeve of his coveralls. Pulling his mind out of the past, he focused very hard on counting out the till. Again. He left three hundred in various coins and bills in the safe for change the next day and put the remaining one grand in a plastic deposit bag, which he would drop at the bank's overnight deposit box on the way home.

As he made his final walk-through to turn off the lights, make sure the AC was off, and double-check that the bays were all closed and locked tight, Rich pulled his phone out of his pocket and read the last few messages from Missy. The most recent simply said, *I love you.*

Even that felt bitter. He wasn't worthy of love. The only reason Missy loved him was because she didn't actually know him.

Rich dropped his head into his hands and dug his palms into his eye sockets. He didn't know where Willa was, hadn't seen her since the night she'd caught him cheating, and he hadn't missed her. He didn't love her anymore. But he still needed her to be okay.

He straightened, squaring his shoulders, and grabbed his backpack and windbreaker. With keys in hand, he was about to head out to his bike when a loud rapping caught his ear.

The front doors were made of glass, so he could look out and see the dark parking lot was empty. The knocking came again. Someone was at the back door. It was pretty common for customers to approach the building that way, given most of the parking was on that side.

Rich sighed and headed to answer, dropping off his stuff on the way. They really needed to post their hours on that door. This wasn't the first time some confused customer had showed up late to pick up a car they'd left for an oil change.

Using his key, he opened the lock and drew the door open. The words *I'm sorry, we're closed* were on the tip of his tongue, but when he saw the person waiting for him, they died in his throat.

The man at the door wore shock-white coveralls, latex gloves, a surgical mask, and big, bug-like goggles. In his hand was a huge drum plug wrench—the one they kept outside near the propane tanks. Nearly a foot long with an adjustable socket on one end, it had to weigh five pounds.

"What are you—"

Rich yelped and scrambled back as the man swung the

wrench, narrowly avoiding the blow. He snatched the edge of the door and tried to slam it closed, but the man stomped his foot onto the threshold to stop it. The attacker threw his shoulder hard against the door, knocking Rich back. His ass smacked into a shop display. Air fresheners and sunglasses clips showered down.

"Wait! Please!" Rich stumbled, frantically trying to find his balance. He snatched the plastic deposit bag from his pocket and threw it at the attacker. "Take the money! Take whatever you want."

The man stepped on the bag as he loomed closer. He raised the wrench again.

Rich turned to run, but the wrench slammed into his shoulder. Pain shot through him like a thousand burning needles. He screamed. The weight and force of the blow drove him to the ground.

"Beg me." The man's voice was harsh as sharp gravel. "Beg me not to kill you."

His shoulder was broken, Rich just knew it. He twisted to face his attacker. "Please! Don't kill me! I'll do anything."

The man raised the wrench again. Before Rich could even scream, heavy metal smashed across his face. The blow sent him spinning. Teeth and blood flew from his mouth.

On his hands and knees, Rich tried to crawl away.

"You killed my daughter." The man's shoes left bloody prints on the tile as he stepped in front of Rich. "You killed her, and you left your girlfriend to take the blame."

Each word landed on Rich like a brick. For a moment, the sounds of the store faded, replaced by the screech of brakes and the memory of headlights that came too late to stop. A child's cry echoed in his ears, piercing, and then silence—an endless, suffocating silence. His chest tightened with guilt as her little face flickered in his mind, frozen in time, forever young.

Because of me.

A few feet away under one of the shop displays, he spotted a screwdriver lying in the dust. If he could get to it, maybe he could fight back. But did he even deserve to?

"You're a piece of shit. The world will be better without you."

"I'm sorry." The apology felt as hollow as it sounded. *Sorry* wouldn't bring this man's daughter back. Choking on the blood oozing between his broken teeth, he inched toward the screwdriver. "It was an accident."

"An accident?" He swooped down and smashed the wrench into the side of Rich's knee, shattering it.

Wild, blinding pain streaked through him. He collapsed flat onto the floor. A moan escaped his throat, an inhuman sound he didn't realize he was capable of making.

"You killed my daughter!" the man shouted again, lifting his weapon for another strike.

"No!" Rich reacted on instinct. He swiveled onto his back and put a hand up to try and stop the blow. The wrench smashed into his face.

"Die!" The heavy tool crashed into his skull, over and over again.

He screamed, trying to fight back—coughing and choking on his own blood and teeth. He thrashed in frantic chaos and blood, until it finally came down across his eyes, rendering him blind.

In one final burst of consciousness, Rich realized his skull had been shattered. The pain pulled him under, deeper and deeper, the little girl's face coming to him again.

I deserve this.

He didn't even attempt to stop the final blow and was glad when the last spark of light and life rushed away from him forever.

21

Winter didn't sleep that night, instead spending every hour reexamining everything she'd collected so far. She reread and replayed every little bit of communication she ever received from Erik Saulson. She stalked Willa York and Rich Benderell's social media, then Missy Stoder's and Chelsea Gray's.

The glut of information was her least favorite thing about any investigation—all the meaningless details she had to sift through before anything resembling a clue jumped out at her. Willa's last post was on January the fifth. And Chelsea had called the police. But this wasn't the first time a missing persons case dried up due to lack of leads.

Noah…

The green shoe they'd found in the bushes was still waiting to be analyzed, but Eve confirmed there was no blood on it. Winter tried to take comfort in that, but it was grasping at invisible threads. Wherever Noah was, he'd been hit by a car. He might be in shock or even developing sepsis or some other infection. She didn't want to think about what else might've been done to him. For the sake of her own sanity, she needed to try to assume the best.

Finding the shoe, especially with no blood, only proved that wherever Noah was, at least one of his feet was cold—and maybe that was the only thing wrong with him.

She prayed he'd been wearing thick socks.

By five a.m., Winter had enough of pretending to rest. She got dressed, shot Eve a text to let her know what she was doing, and headed into the office with nothing in her stomach but a large cup of gas station coffee and the last of Gramma Beth's leftover brownies.

She arrived downtown a little before sunrise and had to park around the block, as the street was closed off for construction. Walking toward her office, Winter froze when she noticed a package at her front door.

A woman walking a Yorkie passed by, offering Winter a jaunty greeting, but she didn't respond. She just stood there, not giving a damn how awkward she looked.

Fear tightened around her bones like a vise. She told herself to keep calm. There was a very good chance Saulson was watching her right at that very moment, delighting in her every reaction. He wanted to see her break, and she still refused to give him the satisfaction.

Closing her eyes, she took a deep breath and approached the door. A white envelope sat on top of a small cardboard box, no bigger than a box of tissues.

Putting her key in the lock, she sidestepped the item and went inside. She went through the motions of hanging up her satchel, setting down her coffee cup, and flicking on the lights. She put her hair back in a tight ponytail and fetched a pair of disposable gloves from her office.

Returning to the front door, Winter picked up the package, carried it inside, and locked the door.

The package was cold to the touch. She resisted the temptation to shake it.

Winter set the box down on her desk and picked up the envelope. Like the others, the flap had simply been tucked, not licked. She unfolded the letter inside, finding the same unremarkable font and formatting. More news from Saulson.

I have a tongue but cannot speak. Tie me up, I'm ready to walk. But if I come undone, you really should stop. What am I?

Winter's lips clenched, and her toes tightened. "A shoe." Of course.

It was everything she could do not to rip the letter into confetti, throw the pieces on the ground, and jump on them like a crazy person until she got blisters.

He was laughing at her, at Noah. Laughing at his shoe. But that wasn't the important takeaway. Erik Saulson was trying to prove he wasn't bluffing about having some kind of contact in law enforcement. Because how the hell else could he know about the shoe? Was he perched in a tree, looking down at them? That wasn't likely, not even for him.

Winter shot a text off to Eve. *Another package from Saulson, and he knows we found the shoe.*

Her reply came almost immediately. *Sit tight, on my way.*

She glanced at the box, dread churning like gravel in her guts. Eve said wait, so she'd wait, though Winter knew the package wasn't going to explode in her face. Saulson was just warming up. Still, she'd been playing by Eve's rules and respected her.

Winter told herself to put the letter down, too, and go make some good coffee, until a foul smell—like rotting hamburger—raided her nasal passage.

The box.

She almost tore it open right then. Instead, she kept reading…

I warned you about involving the cops. I warned you to play by my rules or there would be consequences. I even foreshadowed this for you.

Foreshadowed?

Your progress has been so disappointing.

The smell was overpowering. She set the letter down. What had Saulson foreshadowed?

"Oh, no. Noah's ring. Oh, please, no no no no." Winter choked on her words as sweat prickled her skin. She took out her pocketknife and cut the twine on the cardboard box. The smell of decaying meat intensified.

She pried open the flaps to find several zippered sandwich bags filled with ice. She picked one up, and a scream shot through her throat as she dropped the bag and stood, pushing away from the desk.

In horror, she gazed at the finger lying inside, wrapped in its own tiny bag. A man's finger. And right near where it had been severed, she recognized a tan line from a wedding ring. Hell, she recognized his fingernail.

Winter clambered back farther from her desk, gagging. A putrid taste of coffee and bile filled her throat. Still backing away, she stumbled and sank to her knees.

It was Noah's finger, no doubt. And the wedding band had been Saulson's warm-up stunt to this headliner.

Phantom pains strangled each of her fingers as blood trickled from her nostrils and dripped onto her lips. In her mind's eye, she watched her husband strapped down on his back in the dark, trembling from shock and listening to the steady drip of his own blood as it smacked against cheap vinyl flooring.

If she didn't find him soon, Saulson was going to kill him. He'd said he would and had never once failed to make good on his promises. If she didn't win his stupid game, her husband was as good as dead.

Winter dry-heaved until yellow slime leaked from her mouth onto the hardwood. This couldn't be happening. It was too much. How could any human be expected to handle this? It had to be a nightmare—one of her visions. Just a warning to move faster and work harder before Noah lost his finger.

"Oh, god." She sat down and pulled her knees to her chest, rocking back and forth. This was her fault. She shouldn't have gone to the police, especially knowing he'd warn her not to. Kidnappers always said the same thing. They wanted to keep their victims' families away from the police.

And it was usually foolish to take a psychopath at their word. Except in this case.

Saulson had a pathological need to control the situation. If he was willing to cut Noah's finger if she went to the police, then he was just as likely to do it if she hadn't. His word meant nothing.

Still, if she had listened to him...

Winter clamped her hands to the sides of her head and pulled at her hair. She couldn't do this by herself. And Noah's time was running out.

Tears streaking her face, Winter curled herself into a tight ball, her shoulders shaking with sobs until a knock rattled her door.

22

Eve sat beside Winter at her desk as they reviewed the footage from the office's security cameras. Noah had been right that the angle was a little off and needed some tweaking, but they were still clearly saw a man with floppy, light-colored hair and a gray windbreaker step up to her door and drop off the package.

The time stamp said he'd come at 2:45 a.m.

"Do you know him?" Eve asked, though she knew it was a long shot. The camera was set so high up that the man's face was obscured, only the top of his head clearly visible.

But after dropping off the package, he stopped dead and looked directly into the camera. His eyes were hidden by yellow night-driving glasses, his mouth and nose under a blue surgical mask.

He'd stood like that a long time, the numbers in the corner of the screen counting off the time. At last, he'd shoved his hands in the pockets of his jeans, turned, and walked away.

Winter shook her head and rested her chin on top of her knees. The poor thing was an absolute wreck. Of course she was. Eve didn't want to imagine how she'd react if somebody kidnapped Jackie and started sending bits of him to her in little cardboard boxes. She doubted she could've held herself together as well as Winter was.

She didn't like to think about that, though she'd never been able to help putting herself in other people's shoes, no matter how uncomfortable. If somebody kidnapped her husband, Eve was pretty sure she would've responded with a lot of yelling, violence, and flashing of her badge and gun to intimidate the hell out of anyone she came in contact with.

In fact, these last two nights when she'd gotten home, she'd woken her husband up just so she could hug him really hard and tell him how grateful she was that he never went jogging.

He told her she was welcome. *"Just for you, I'm not going to go jogging again tomorrow."*

She'd started to laugh, but it quickly transformed into unshed tears and sobs that caught in her throat like stinging nettles. Her husband wrapped her in his arms and held her tight until they both fell asleep.

Winter clicked back to the beginning to play the footage of the delivery person over again. "He's probably just another of Saulson's lackeys."

Eve scowled at that—not because it was unlikely, but because it was so annoying. "How the hell does this dude get so many people to work for him? Do you think he's independently wealthy or what?"

Winter shrugged. Her face was splotchy, eyes dry and red as if she'd run out of tears. "Maybe. Most likely. But I think his main currency is secrets."

Eve turned to her. "How do you mean?"

"That's how he controlled Cybil Kerie. After he got her to confide in him, he went about making her darkest desire come true, embroiling her in criminal wrongdoing in the process. By the time she wanted out, it was too late."

Eve nodded and got up from her chair. "Let's ID this little guy, okay?"

"It's Noah's. I know it is. I know what his hands look like, his fingers, his ears…" Winter pulled her chair up close to her computer and clicked open a browser.

Eve read the words she typed in the search bar. *How long can you still reattach severed fingers?*

Eve picked up the cardboard box. "I'm just gonna take this to the break room for a minute, okay?"

"Be careful with it." Winter's blue eyes were as sharp and serious as a surgeon's blade.

"I promise." With gloved hands, Eve carried the box to the break room and set it down on the kitchen counter.

She carefully removed the bagged finger, only to discover a note sealed in a bag under it.

"Winter's gonna love this," she said to herself. "First things first."

Pressing the bluish flesh of the finger pad into the baggie to make it tight and clear, she snapped a picture.

Satisfied by the quality of the print, Eve accessed the national database and uploaded her photo. Then she pulled up Noah's prints—beginning with his left ring finger—and told the program to compare them.

The match came back almost instantly. This was Noah's finger.

Eve carefully put the finger back in the box and placed a baggie of ice on top. She had a strong sense Winter wanted the finger near her, so she carried the box, along with the note, back into the office and set it back down next to her.

"The timeline to reattach a finger is ideally within six hours, but it could potentially be reattached within twenty-four hours." Winter summarized what she'd found on the internet. "And apparently putting it directly on ice is not a good idea. It can damage the tissues."

At least Saulson had packaged the finger correctly. Eve tried to think of something useful to say—anything that would sound helpful or insightful. All that came out was, "Shit."

"If we took it to the hospital, maybe they could preserve it somehow. They have to be able to do something to keep it viable a little longer until we can get Noah back."

That sounded like a stretch. The finger was all they had of Noah right now—the only part of him Winter might feel able to save. With her eyes still trained on the monitor, she reached out and set her hand on top of the box. The touch was gentle and affectionate, like a wife laying her hand on her husband's knee.

It hurt to watch—a sucker punch straight to Eve's heart. Even if it was a little gross to see how attached Winter was to it.

Eve pressed her lips together, considering. If someone cut off Jackie's finger, she would want to keep it. Like a bloody, slowly rotting security blanket.

Ew.

On second thought, she didn't like the way Winter was touching the box. She was sick with worry about her husband, and that was causing her to grasp at straws. Slowly but surely, she was falling away from reality. Noah needed them both firmly on solid ground. There was no time for emotional comfort phalanges.

"I hate to pile on, but…" Eve set the note encased in a baggie in front of Winter. "It was under Noah's finger."

Winter didn't even need to take it out of the bag to read it. "'Where does TED go swimming?'" She looked at Eve. "Who the hell is TED?"

"I wish I knew."

Eve gestured to the box containing Noah's finger. "I'm going to take this to the FBI offices. I'll talk to our M.E. and see if he has any ideas of what we can do to try to keep it viable longer. But we can't waste our time worrying about a finger. We have to save the rest of Noah. And I'll have them analyze this for prints or any kind of DNA." She picked up the note with the riddle about TED going swimming.

Winter nodded, still wincing as she read on her computer.

Without warning, she jumped up from the desk and punched the wall behind her. "Fuck you, Saulson!"

The sheetrock gave out, and Winter's fist left a big hole.

"When I find that son of a bitch, he's going to wish he'd never heard of me. Or Noah. Or Justin. I'm gonna cut everything off him!" She punched the wall again, opening up yet another hole. When she pulled her hand back, her knuckles were red and scraped.

Eve's first instinct was to remind Winter that it would be illegal to retaliate against Erik Saulson with violence, no matter what he did. But Winter knew that. She would never actually cut anything off another living person.

Would she?

She didn't know Winter well enough to say for certain, but she was coming to appreciate why Noah was so obsessed with keeping his wife safe. Somebody quite literally *had* to do it. Never mind that there was just something about Winter Black. Her passion was infectious. Eve would've been ashamed to admit it out loud, but working with Winter and looking for Noah was the most alive she'd felt in years.

"He wants me to play his game." Winter dropped back into her office chair and spun around to her computer. The moment her fingers touched the keys, she began typing furiously. "I'll play, you fuck. I'll win too. I always win in the end. I'm going to destroy you."

Eve shivered and picked up the box. She stood watching her for a little while longer, but Winter was gone—absorbed in her work. Her obsession.

"I'm heading out now." Eve wanted to hug her but suppressed the urge. "Call me before you do anything."

Winter grunted but didn't look up.

Taking the noise for acquiescence, Eve stepped out of the office and onto the sidewalk. Years of training that started in her family long before she officially joined the Agency kept Eve even-tempered and calm in stressful situations, but as soon as she was outside, her heart rate began to pick up. The box felt so heavy in her hands, and she was very careful not to let it shift. She wasn't sure she'd be able to handle the feeling with vomit rising in her throat.

When she reached her SUV, Eve gently laid the box on her passenger seat, closed the door, and leaned her body against it. She sucked breath through her teeth. When she closed her eyes, all she could see was Noah—the big badass teddy bear she'd come to care for so much, though they'd been partners for such a brief time. She didn't want to imagine him screaming or thrashing or negotiating for his life, but better that than…than the alternative.

Clenching a fist, Eve swallowed hard and stuffed all her stupid feelings back into her intestines, where they belonged. Winter wasn't going to sleep until they found Noah, so Eve wouldn't either. They would find Noah, whatever it took. Even if Winter ended up chopping a few choice bits off Erik Saulson.

If it came to that, Eve might just have to look the other way.

23

Stuck in traffic again, Winter scribbled on a notebook pressed against her steering wheel. Cobbling together testimony from Missy Stoder, Chelsea Gray, and Rich Benderell, and adding that to what little the police had gathered, she'd constructed a loose timeline of the night Willa York disappeared.

Willa came home unexpectedly—about seven p.m.—and caught Rich and Missy together.

They'd had a big blowout. According to the neighbor, Thatcher Templeton, Rich stormed out and went down to the parking lot, where he paced for a while.

Waiting to attack Willa? Waiting for something or someone? Or simply cooling down before driving away? And allegedly smoking.

She drew a circle around his name, looping it again and again. He was hiding something. Something that left his eyes looking like black water in a moonless night—empty and so very lonely.

Willa packed and then left in a hurry, alone. Later that night, a security camera captured her entering The Travelers Tavern and then leaving. Both times, she was alone.

Was she meeting anyone? Did anyone see her? Had she simply gone to the bar for a drink to cool down? The time stamps on the CCTV printouts suggested Willa wasn't in the bar for long, about two hours.

Winter navigated the Pilot through several more blocks of traffic before pulling up to the bar. She'd get answers to those questions right now.

The joint was hopping with the lunch crowd. A big banner out front advertised a $14.95 soup, sandwich, and beer special.

Had Winter eaten yet today? She couldn't remember. Whereas yesterday, she'd simply been too distracted to remember her basic bodily needs, now the very idea of putting food in her mouth and chewing made her feel like she might get sick all over the concrete.

How long had it been since she'd remembered to have a glass of water? At least since the last time Eve made her drink one.

Stepping into the busy building, Winter dodged past the diners sitting at small, round, steel-topped tables and headed straight for the bar. She ordered a glass of ice water and drank the whole thing before calling the bartender back over.

"Excuse me?"

"You ready to order, hon?" The young woman rested her hand on the bar, elbow cocked at an awkward angle, so Winter got a clear view of her huge Winnie-the-Pooh tattoo.

"I'm here investigating the disappearance of young woman who was last seen at this bar three months ago."

"Oh, crap." The woman wiped down the counter with a rough rag and leaned in closer, her diamond-stud nose ring winking in the lamplight. "That's not good. I guess that means y'all ain't found her yet?"

"Did you speak to the police already?"

"Yeah, they were in here yesterday talking to Charlie, my boss."

"Which officer came to speak with you? Do you remember their name?"

"He said he was a detective. Lister? I think."

"Lessner?"

"Sounds about right."

She was glad someone was still following leads on the case, but Winter thought Darnell said he was taking over, according to Eve. She'd have to call him, see if he got caught up in the court hearing for the Railroad Killer.

Winter studied the ceiling, scanning for distinctive little boxes and seeing nothing. "I was wondering if you have any cameras inside the bar, and if I could get a look at the footage."

"Like Charlie told Lister, we have zero cameras inside. He's kinda old-fashioned that way. Big libertarian, anti-Big Brother but believes in bigfoot kinda guy, you know? We got the old black-and-white on the front door, but that's it."

She cursed internally. "Could you help me get in contact with whoever was working on Tuesday, January fifth?"

"Yeah, um. Sure." She grabbed a clipboard on the back wall, flipping to a buried page. "I was here. Tuesday is kind of a crapshoot. It gets real busy if there's a game going on in the stadium down the street. Other times it's dead. We had a big birthday party that night. Otherwise, I dunno. It kind of all blurs together."

Winter tried to pluck anything useful from what she was saying. "And?"

"I told the cop to look at our Insta, but I don't know if he knew what I was talking about." The bartender pointed at a sign over the counter that bore a hashtag, *#AustinTravelersTavern*. "Somebody might've caught your missing girl in one of their pictures. When you use the hashtag, you're entered into a drawing where you can win prizes like free drinks, free plays on the jukebox, and gift certificates. We have a few regulars who are really into it."

Winter took her phone out of her pocket, went into the app store, and started the download. She didn't have Insta or any other social media on her phone. Enough people constantly violated her privacy without her inviting them to do it.

She made a throwaway account and searched for the tavern's hashtag. Photos populated immediately, and she scrolled back toward the correct date.

Perhaps sensing that their conversation was at an end, the bartender drifted away to attend to customers. Winter turned her back to the bar and hunched over her phone.

The photos from that night mainly showed the aforementioned birthday party. There were balloons in the shape of the number thirty, a small pile of presents, and a lot of pictures of a redheaded woman with a huge, Julia Roberts grin.

She scrolled for the photos, ignoring everything that wasn't Willa York. She found a photo of the redheaded birthday girl posing with her boyfriend. He'd pulled her in close for a sloppy kiss on the cheek while she laughed… revealing a woman with a black pixie cut sitting at the bar with her back to the camera.

Thorns sprang in Winter's gut. All her life, she'd always hated mushy crap. Rom-coms, poetry, Valentine's Day. She never cared about any of it and rolled her eyes at people who lamented being single. She'd always assumed that—given how screwed up she was—she'd live and die alone. And she'd been fine with that. Until she met Noah, and he slowly but surely weaseled his way into her heart. The thought of life without him was unimaginable.

A tear pooled in the corner of her eye and slipped down her cheek.

"No," she whispered, closing her eyes to take a steadying breath. "You're not allowed to be sad, dammit. You have to stay mad. You have to keep fighting."

She clenched her teeth so hard, it hurt, fanning the painful flames in her belly.

The people at the birthday party had taken about six thousand photos, and a few showed Willa York. In one photo, her face was turned toward the camera. She looked angry and tired and blotchy, which made perfect sense, given what had happened to her just an hour before the photo was taken.

Willa seemed to be talking to a man standing at her side in one of the photos. His back was to the camera, so all she could see was his shoulder and his arm in the air over the bar, ordering a drink. A big red patch of skin showed on his wrist where the cuff of his jacket was pulled back. It looked like a burn or maybe a very ugly tattoo. She couldn't tell.

Flicking through more pictures, she realized Willa hadn't been with the man. But in most of the photos, she'd been facing the person sitting to her other side.

And there it was. A hand on Willa's back. One placed there out of comfort. The hand belonged to a Caucasian woman—and there, starting on the pinky and curving down around her wrist, was a tattoo of roses on a vine.

Willa's roommate, Chelsea Gray. Yet Chelsea had said the last time they saw one another was at the apartment before Willa stormed out.

Chelsea had lied. This picture confirmed she was actually the last person to see Willa alive that night.

Winter's phone rang in her hand. Detective Davenport. "Darnell?"

"I've got an update for you on Willa York." His voice was

as deep and emotionless as ever. In the background was a commotion of voices and the vague, high-low song of a siren.

Acid bubbled up Winter's esophagus. Always, she tried to keep herself from leaping to conclusions—a very dangerous jump to make in her profession—but she could hardly help the first thought that came into her head. "You found her body?"

Normally, she would've kept such a question to herself, but her brain-to-mouth filter was one of many nonessential functions she couldn't be bothered to utilize in her current, half-broken state.

"We found a body, but it's not Willa York's."

"What do you mean?"

"Her ex-boyfriend, Rich Benderell. Murdered."

24

Winter darted through the crowd of the busy tavern, not giving a crap when she bumped into people with her shoulders and knocked them out of the way. "How'd he die? What happened?"

"Can't confirm that just yet. The scene is the victim's place of work, Pinsky's Auto. We're pretty sure we have the murder weapon. A drum plug wrench."

Throwing open her SUV door, Winter got behind the wheel. She put the call on speaker, opened her maps app, and pulled up the address of Haven House Apartments. "What's that, exactly?"

"A big wrench used for opening barrels. It belongs to the shop. We think the killer picked it up outside. Weighs about five pounds."

"Rich was beaten to death?" Winter fired up the engine and peeled out of the parking lot, nearly hitting a Chevy on her way out. The man behind the wheel shouted something rude at her, which she ignored completely.

"Afraid so. The scene's a mess." Davenport sounded

thoroughly disgusted, his voice making her jump as the call automatically transferred to her vehicle's speakers. She turned the volume down and tossed her phone into the cup holder.

That wasn't a good sign. It took a lot to gross out your average homicide detective.

The road lay before her, but instead, she saw Rich Benderell sitting on the floor of the auto shop, a little streak of oil on his forehead, looking so broken.

He'd been keeping something from her. Something about Willa. Something she knew deep in her gut was very important. Now she might never find out what that something was.

"Lessner went to The Travelers Tavern."

"Okay?"

"I guess nothing. I just thought you took over the case."

"I did. I am." Everything Darnell said was sounding like a question.

"You need to call Eve."

"You mean Taggart?"

"Yes. Ask her what happened this morning."

"O-kay..." He sang the vowels low and slow. "Is there some reason you can't tell me?"

Winter almost answered, but her mouth was too dry. She snatched her water bottle from the center console and sucked on the straw.

Empty.

"Winter?"

"I can't talk about it. Just call Eve, okay? But don't say a word to anybody else. You aren't speaking to me, and you're not getting any information from me."

He sighed. She could see the exhausted roll of his eyes and dubious rubbing of his cropped hair as if he were sitting right next to her. "You still think there's a rat in the department?"

"I *know* there is. I just don't know who or what. It doesn't even have to be a person, necessarily. Saulson has proven he knows his way around a computer, or at least, he has lackeys who do. If he finds out I'm working with you, there will be consequences."

"What consequences? What are you talking about?"

Bile congealed in her throat, catching her breath. "Just call Eve."

Winter disconnected the call and gripped the steering wheel with all her strength.

Her brain zoned out, so she drove the ten miles to Chelsea and Missy's apartment complex on autopilot.

As Winter arrived, a young father was struggling to push his clunky stroller through the entrance. After graciously holding the door for the father and child, Winter slipped inside without having to let anyone know she was there.

Passing through the lobby toward the elevators, she spotted Thatcher Templeton standing at the mailboxes. His disheveled yellow hair looked different to her today than it had yesterday.

He was the right height, the right build. If she put him in a blue windbreaker and some sunglasses, he easily could've been the man who came by her office and left that hideous package.

She stepped forward and cleared her throat.

Thatcher turned toward her, deftly closing the brass door of his mail cubby. "Oh, hello again."

"Hello." Winter pushed the button on the elevator to go up.

He stepped up beside her. "How's the investigation coming along?"

"It's coming."

"I wanted to mention, I went over to talk to Missy and Chelsea last night to express my concern for Willa."

The elevator doors dinged open, and they both stepped inside. He pushed the button to take them to the correct floor. Standing in such close quarters, Winter couldn't help noticing the scent of spices and grease coming from his clothing. Like the food in the tavern, it churned her stomach with an urge to vomit.

She sidestepped to move away.

"I don't think they actually care about her at all." His fingers tightened on the glossy catalog in his hands. "Honestly, Willa was the only one of the three I ever liked. I have more compassion in my little toe than either of those other little bitches have in their whole bodies."

Winter flinched at his vitriol. She could easily imagine the scene. Thatcher knocking on their door, trying to engage the women in conversation, not realizing they both found him creepier than English ivy.

"Willa was a beautiful person," he continued. "Kind and open and decent. Nothing like those other two. Why is it always the pure souls who are taken from this world too soon? And why are so many evil people allowed to linger?"

Winter had to force her hand not to creep toward her concealed sidearm. Talking about a missing person in the past tense was a massive, waving, glow-in-the-dark red flag. Why the hell was Thatcher Templeton so interested in Willa York anyway? She'd found no indication that they shared any kind of real friendship. People who actually loved a missing person tended to cling to hope far past the point when police were statistically likely to find them alive.

She smiled gently, careful to wrinkle the skin around her eyes so that it looked genuine. "Thank you for your concern. Might I swing by later to ask you a few more questions?"

"I guess so, though I don't know how much help I would be."

The doors dinged and whooshed open. With her arms tight at her sides, Winter rushed out before Thatcher. She'd deal with him later. Right now, she had another liar on her list, and she wasn't going to let herself get distracted.

She waited in the hall until the man opened his door and disappeared inside. Only then did she knock on Chelsea and Missy's apartment door.

As she waited, she checked her phone. Eve would be calling any minute.

The door inched open, and Chelsea peeked through the crack. "Oh, it's you." She closed the door, undid a chain latch, and pulled it all the way open. "I thought you were the cops again."

"Have the police been here?"

Chelsea wrapped her arms around her chest as if she were cold. "They just left."

"I guess that means you heard about Rich?"

She nodded, her lips hanging open like a lost goldfish. "Missy's supposed to be headed down to the station for a longer interview with them."

"Is she home now?"

Chelsea nodded. "She's a mess. I just got her into the shower. When the cops came by to tell her what happened, she dropped her coffee all over herself. We're gonna need to rent a cleaner to get it up, I think."

"Do you mind if I ask you a few more questions?"

She glanced toward the hall. "Not at all. C'mon into the kitchen. I was just making some candles."

Winter followed her through the living room into the kitchen. A smell of bergamot and frankincense permeated the air. Cream-colored wax bubbled in a pot on the stove. Chelsea hurried closer and turned down the flame.

"I want to go back to the last time you saw Willa." Winter fully expected Chelsea to lie, so she watched her carefully. "Here at the apartment, right?"

"Uh-huh." Her back was to Winter as she stirred the wax.

"How long were Missy and Rich seeing one another behind Willa's back?"

"I think like six months?" She picked up what looked like a chopstick, wrapped some white string around it, and dangled it into a decorative teacup. "They hooked up the night we all went to see Wiz Khalifa, whenever that was."

Winter moved so that she could at least see Chelsea's profile. "So you knew they were together the whole time and never told Willa?"

Chelsea bit her lip, looking guilty. "It was awful having to keep the secret from her. Missy kept saying she was going to tell her the truth, but Rich refused to break up with Willa."

"Why?"

She picked up the pot of wax, gently poured it into the teacup, and set about dangling the wick for another. "I don't know. He kept saying it wasn't the right time. He just wanted more time."

"More time for what?"

"To grow a pair, if you ask me." Chelsea set down the pot and turned to Winter. "It was really weird, because, like, it was so obvious he loved Missy. And he was clearly miserable with Willa, but he refused to do anything about it. And then they got caught."

Winter's brain pulsed with short staccato thoughts like the taps of Morse code. *Missy loves Rich. Rich won't break up with Willa. Missy decides to get rid of Willa. Rich finds out and he threatens to expose Missy. To cover her tracks, Missy kills Rich too.*

She already knew Chelsea lied about where she was the night Willa went missing, which meant both she and Missy had no alibi.

It was a solid theory. There was only one problem. Where did Erik Saulson fit into any of that? She knew he'd been involved in Willa's disappearance, regardless of who might've done the actual deed. She knew because of the Cybil Kerie and Dr. Poole connection.

Winter wasn't quite ready to straight-up accuse anybody just yet. She'd throw out a few more vague lines first and hope she caught something. "Missy must've been kind of relieved when Willa accidentally caught them together."

Chelsea stretched her neck from side to side, popping it. "Well, that wasn't exactly an accident."

"What do you mean?"

"What the hell is she doing here?" Missy snarled from the doorway. She had a towel around her hair and was dressed in loose sweatpants and a paint-stained t-shirt with a picture of a motorcycle on it. The words under the graphic read *Bikesexual, I'll ride anything*.

"I heard what happened to Rich. I'm so sorry."

Missy stalked past her to the coffeepot on the counter. "You wanna ask me about Rich too? 'Cause I've already told the cops everything, and now I've got to go down to the station and tell them again."

"That's standard procedure with a homicide. People tend to be killed by those closest to them, so the cops have to eliminate friends and family before they can look at anyone else."

"I would never hurt Rich!" Missy whirled, the coffeepot shaking in her hand. "I loved him. He was my everything. I—"

Her hands quivered. She started to cry. Winter needed to get the hell out of there before all that profound sadness soaked into her skin like poison.

Stay mad, she told herself. *Stay useful.*

"So it wasn't an accident that Willa walked in on you and Rich?"

Missy's face snapped to Chelsea, daggers in her eyes. "You told her?"

"I didn't. I—"

"Yeah, so what?" Missy turned back to Winter. "We knew she was planning on coming back early. Rich knew."

"That's certainly one way to send a message." Winter wasn't here to sermonize, but that sounded needlessly cruel. "You couldn't have had a conversation with her? Written her a letter?"

"It needed to be persuasive. Otherwise, she would've wheedled her way back to Rich." Missy's dagger eyes stabbed Winter. "I don't need your lecture. The breakup needed to happen, one way or the other. It was better than continuing to live a lie with a man who couldn't stand her."

That sounded an awful lot like a moral question, which Winter didn't have time for right now. It also sounded like pretty compelling motivation for murder.

Erik Saulson didn't call himself *the Watcher* for nothing. He had targeted Willa to open a vacancy at Dr. Ava Poole's office, but he didn't want to get his own hands dirty. Instead, he started digging into Willa, searching for someone who had reason to want her gone. Was it Rich? Missy? She couldn't picture Chelsea as the culprit, despite the fact that she'd lied.

"So Willa never saw it coming?"

"She sure seemed surprised, unless blabbermouth here warned her."

"I didn't say anything," Chelsea mumbled. She was back to paying attention to her candles, her head down and shoulders slumped.

It was clear who was the dominant one in this friendship.

"You must've felt guilty after keeping that kind of secret

from your friend for so long. Is that why you went with her to the bar that night?"

"What the hell are you talking about?" Missy scoffed. "I didn't go anywhere with Willa."

"I wasn't talking to you."

Missy did a double take before her gaze latched onto Chelsea. "What's she talking about, Chels?"

"Um…" Chelsea poured the wax for another teacup candle, very deliberately keeping her focus on the cup. "Well, I might have. I just wanted to make sure she was okay."

"You little traitor!"

"That's not fair. You and Willa are both my friends. It's your fault I had to lie to her for so long, which I did. I never said a word."

Winter was quick to cut in, not wanting the conversation to devolve into an argument until she had everything she needed and was out the door. "So you did meet her at the bar?"

Chelsea set the pot down and turned off the burner. "I called her, and she told me where she was, so I went there to try to talk to her. I wanted to be there for her and help her through things. I tried to make her see how unhappy she and Rich had been for so long."

"Did she not take that well?"

"She yelled at me. Told me I was just as guilty as Missy for lying to her about everything. Called me a few choice names. I tried to stay calm and asked her where she was going to stay that night. I tried to convince her to just come back home. I knew she didn't have anywhere to go." Her shoulders slumped. "But she wouldn't listen to anything I said. I sat there for a while until I finally gave up."

"Were you drinking?"

Chelsea nodded. "I bought us a round of shots. Willa had already had a couple by the time I came in."

"Did you notice her talking to anyone else?"

"No, she was just sitting by herself and drinking."

"Why didn't you mention this last time I was here?"

Chelsea shot a telling glance at Missy. "'Cause it wasn't important. Nothing happened. Finally, I went to pee and when I came back, she was gone. I ran out into the parking lot, and she was backing her car out. I was still basically sober, but she wouldn't let me take her anywhere or get out of her car, so I followed her. After she pulled up to a motel and walked into the office, I thought she'd be safe from there, so I left."

"What motel?"

"The Magary Motel by the highway on Whistler Street. Real dump."

Winter couldn't help sermonizing again. "You didn't think this was vital information? A woman has gone missing. You have to tell the cops the whole truth about what happened that night." She jabbed her finger first at Chelsea, then at Missy. "Both of you. If you don't, I will. And that won't look good for either of you. Do you understand?"

Chelsea looked down, like a little girl getting lectured, and nodded.

"Missy, when I asked before, you said you and Chelsea were together all that night. Do you want to tell me now where you really were?"

Missy's nostrils flared with righteous indignation. "We were both here, and then I went over to Rich's house." Her voice cracked on his name.

So Rich lied too. He wasn't alone. Except I can't interrogate him again.

"I waited for a bit, and he never showed, so I came back home. That's it." Her angry veneer had fallen away to reveal broken sadness underneath. Maybe she was innocent of everything except infidelity. Maybe she really loved Rich and was heartbroken over losing him.

Or what seemed to be sadness could be regret and guilt over what she'd done. Or she could simply be faking it.

"And she came home a little bit later." Missy swung a thumb in her roommate's direction, refusing to look at her.

"I really wasn't with Willa very long." Chelsea shrugged.

"One last thing before I go," Winter said. "What was the relationship between Willa and your neighbor, Mr. Templeton?"

The two women looked at one another at the mention of his name, sharing a subtle twitch of disgust.

"What *relationship*?" Missy's lip curled into a sneer. "You mean how he was always staring at her?"

"And inventing excuses to talk to her?"

"The way he'd wait by the mailboxes for her to come down just so he could corner her?"

Winter couldn't believe the women hadn't mentioned this before but kept the anger from her voice. "Was he stalking her?"

"I don't know if he was *stalking*." Chelsea shrugged. "Willa's a really friendly, outgoing person. She talks to everyone. He definitely creeped her out, though."

"He creeps everybody out. He's a freak." Missy shuddered. "He's the one you and the cops should be looking into."

"Why's that?"

Missy twitched her nose, hesitating. "I heard he used to have a wife and a daughter. Then, one day, they just disappeared."

"He works in a funeral home," Chelsea added, as if that was supposed to mean something profound.

"Are you implying he might've done something to harm his wife and daughter?"

Missy lifted her shoulders. "I don't know anything, except he lives alone and nobody ever comes to visit him."

"He was kind of obsessed with Willa." Chelsea's eyes widened, and her jaw dropped. "Oh, my god. Do you think he did something to her?"

"I don't know." Winter started for the door. "But I'm going to find out."

25

Back at her office, Winter called Darnell and told him about The Magary Motel, Willa's last known whereabouts.

"I'll send a team to comb the scene right now."

With that handled, she did a deep dive into Thatcher Montgomery Templeton. His fingerprints were everywhere on the internet. The first thing she learned was that he hosted a popular blog on the subject of cryptozoology—the Loch Ness Monster, the Jersey Devil, and so very many ghosts.

He wrote at length about his work in the mortuary—the things he would hear and see late at night when he was alone with the bodies. He wrote books, too, including a compilation of his essays, now featuring an expanded introduction for the tenth anniversary edition. This new and updated edition had thousands of four- and five-star reviews on Amazon.

Her curiosity piqued, Winter took the time to read part of his latest entry—a write-up on a mythical kind of worm that supposedly lived in the Rocky Mountains and had the ability to eat and break down nuclear waste.

She was surprised to find she enjoyed his writing—clear, concise, intelligent, and dripping with tongue-in-cheek humor, all while respecting the seriousness of his subject. In fact, his writing was so charming, it was hard for her to believe the guy online was the same person she'd met at the apartment complex.

It was possible that all his creepiness stemmed from the fact that he was just a bit shy. Or that it was just a mask he wore to hide the monster inside.

She clicked the links on his website that took her back to his social media. Virtually everything he posted was just recycled content from his blogs—little snippets to try to get people into his funnel. It all led back to his books, his Patreon, and his members-only cryptid-hunting club.

Closing the blog, Winter opened her Tracers program and searched his name.

Thatcher was born and raised in Austin. Fifteen years ago, he married another mortician, and they ran their own funeral home together until they divorced eight years later. She'd thought it was odd that a mortician would be renting—the money was great, and business was always booming—but a little digging revealed his wife had kept the business in their divorce. It seemed he'd been focused more on his writing since then.

He and his ex-wife had one daughter together, who was marked as deceased.

Recalling her first conversation with him, when he mentioned his daughter, Winter's tender heart began to bleed. Empathetic sadness led to a crash of deep, personal sadness. She thought of Noah tied up somewhere, bleeding and all alone. Every moment suffering excruciating pain as he waited for her or anybody to come for him.

Just as she was about to search the cause of the daughter's death, a painful sob smacked her in the back, knocking the breath from her lungs. She began to cry, her breath growing shallower and shallower.

Winter punched her fist onto the desk, making her laptop hop. "Stop it. Knock it off."

Snatching up a tissue, she wiped her eyes and dropped it on the floor. Noah couldn't afford for her to freak out right now. She had to stay sharp.

She put her phone on speaker and called Eve, her eyes glued to her computer screen as she waited through the rings.

"What's up, babe?"

"I need you to look something up for me."

"Shoot."

Winter gave her the names of the Templetons and other relevant info. "I'm pretty sure the daughter died a number of years ago. Can you look into that for me?"

"I'm on it."

A dull ache pounded in the back of Winter's head. She picked up Saulson's most recent letter from the corner of her desk and read it again. "I'm so sick of these games."

"No doubt, but that seems to be all the man cares about. He thinks he's freaking Lex Luthor or something."

"Kidnapped a damn FBI agent, and I can't involve the authorities. So unreasonable."

"I've never read the *Sicko Stalker Freak Rulebook*, but I'm gonna guess *be reasonable* isn't written anywhere in it."

"Well, if you get a copy, send it my way. I can't take much more of this. I feel like I'm going crazy."

"Screw his rules," Eve spat. "What we need are the damn cheat codes."

Winter let out a sigh so heavy, she deflated along with it, resting her crown against the edge of her desk. "'Where does TED go swimming?'"

"Could TED be this Thatcher guy? Is 'Ted' a nickname for Thatcher?"

"I guess it could be." Winter chewed on her lip. Suddenly, she felt so tired. Her empty stomach grumbled unhappily. "TED was all in uppercase, though. It makes me think it isn't a name."

"Could it be a TED Talk? Something about swimming?"

Winter's stomach growled again. "I don't know. TED Talks are generally so uplifting. And he's so not."

"I don't know if we should focus on grammar so much."

"Saulson pays attention to detail. I think it means something. Clearly, it is very important to him to seem clever."

"I googled TED and swimming and got a talk about building your resilience with open water swimming. Is that like in the ocean?"

"We're nowhere near the ocean." Winter thumped her forehead against her desk in frustration, but immediately regretted it, as the ache in the back of her brain intensified. "Where do people go swimming in Austin? You've lived here a long time, right? Where do you go swimming?"

"Uh, okay. Wimberley is always fun. Me and Jack take the kids there sometimes. That's a drive, though. Mostly we just go to the pool."

Pool.

The word sent a bolt of electricity down Winter's spine, forcing her to straighten in her seat. "What did you just say?"

"What, Wimberley?"

"You said you go to the pool."

"Did you figure it out?"

"I don't know who the hell TED is," Winter slapped her laptop closed and rose to her feet, a satisfied smile lifting her cracked lips, "but I do know someone named Poole."

26

When Winter arrived at Blue Tree Wellness Center, Dr. Poole was with a patient.

"It should only be another ten minutes or so, if you'd like to wait." The receptionist, the young man with the magnificent beard, took an eight-ounce bottle of water from the tiny fridge behind him and offered it to Winter.

"Thanks." Cracking the bottle open, Winter drained it all in a few loud gulps and tossed it into a wicker recycling bin.

Far too anxious to sit and wait, she paced and flicked her fingers.

"Where does TED go swimming?"

As usual, she and the receptionist were alone in the large waiting room—him at one end, her the other—so she didn't worry about anyone watching her.

She plucked the latest copy of *People* from the magazine rack and flicked through it, searching for any stories about Ted Danson, Ted Nugent, Ted Cruz…Ted Bundy.

Nothing. She snatched up a *National Geographic*. Then *Vogue*. Then *Popular Mechanics*. She read half of an article written by a Ted Raglan about the U.S. Army's newest tank technology.

Nothing, nothing, nothing.

Winter drummed her fingers in frustration. The clock on the wall seemed to be moving in reverse. Poole would know who or what "TED" was. She had to. Part of Winter wanted to just barge into the doctor's session and demand answers. The only reason she didn't was that pissing Poole off might make it harder to pull useful information from her.

Winter's chest deflated, and she collapsed into a chair, suddenly tired. Her eyes zoned out in the direction of the oil on canvas painting directly ahead. It really was soothing, like everything else in Poole's waiting area. Fluffy trees in soft greens with a trail winding through them, a lilac sky with those little M-shaped birds in flight.

It looked like an original done by a talented amateur artist, of a local park, possibly. Maybe one of Poole's patients had made it for her. Winter's attention drifted to the lower right corner of the painting for a signature.

In clean black brushstrokes, the name spelled out *TED*.

Winter jumped from her chair and stumbled closer until her nose nearly touched the letters.

A park? A nature preserve? What the hell was Saulson trying to tell her?

Without a second thought, Winter grabbed the canvas from its wall mount and flipped it over.

"Hey," the receptionist objected weakly. "You can't do that."

Winter ignored him.

The back was blank. She searched for flaws, hidden compartments, secret writing.

The door to Dr. Poole's office opened, and she and a small man with Coke-bottle glasses stepped out. She looked at

Winter, confusion registering subtly on her face, before turning to her patient.

"Thank you, Gregory, I'll see you next time."

"Okay." The little man walked by the office, taking a wide arc around Winter and giving her a look like she was an escaped mental patient.

"Winter?" Dr. Poole approached slowly, removing a pair of glasses Winter had never seen her wear before. "What are you doing?"

"Where did you get this?"

"Do you like it?" Dr. Poole smiled in that vaguely parental way that doctors loved. "I'll be happy to tell you all about it. Come on back."

Winter glanced at the wall, then at the painting, then back again.

"You can bring it with you, if you like."

She did want to bring it with her. Sucking on her bottom lip, Winter followed Dr. Poole past the reception desk into her office.

"Who's TED?"

"I'm sorry?"

Winter set the oil painting down on the sofa and pointed to the initials in the corner. "*T. E. D.* Who is he?" She took out her phone. "May I?" She gestured with her camera pointed toward the image.

"Sure." Poole smiled gently. "And that painting was a gift from one of my patients many years ago, when I first opened my practice. His name was Thom Dross. Edwin or Edward or something was his middle name."

Winter's head bobbed like an impatient quail as she snapped a couple of photos and waited for the doctor to continue. "And?"

"And...he was a very sweet man."

"Was?"

"He passed a few years back."

"Where was he from?"

"Austin, I think. Or at least, he'd lived here for a very long time. That painting was done somewhere in Dick Nichols Park, if I'm not much mistaken."

"Dick Nichols…" Winter had never heard of it, but that was unsurprising, since she'd lived in Austin such a short time. She whipped out her phone to look it up. It looked pretty big, with lots of trees and trails, as well as a rec center.

And the park had a pool. Was that significant?

Phone in hand, Winter took several pictures of the painting. Maybe she could find the place by examining the curves of trails and branches.

"What is this all about? You look, um…tired, Winter. Can I offer you some water?"

Winter shook her head.

"Is this painting connected to Willa?"

"It better be." Turning sharply on her heel, Winter started for the office door. Her phone said it would take forty minutes to get to the park—more time stuck in traffic, more twitching.

"Wait." Dr. Poole followed her, though with her clicky kitten heels and restrictive pencil skirt, she was no match for Winter's stride. "There's something I need to tell you!"

"What?" Winter pivoted, her silky black hair falling over a shoulder from the momentum.

"The police came to talk to me about Willa this morning." Dr. Poole bowed her head, seemingly too heavy for her thin neck. She stared at her patent leather heels a moment before meeting Winter's gaze. "Well, her boyfriend. I'm sure you heard what happened to him."

Winter nodded solemnly. "Do you remember the officer's name?"

"Detective Davenport. I liked him a lot better than that

short, slimy detective who arrested me." She frowned like a kid trying to swallow a raw oyster.

She was talking about Lessner. Winter almost said she liked Darnell better, too, but didn't want to accidentally undermine the investigation or anybody involved with it.

"Did Davenport ask you a question that sparked your memory?"

"Yes. Many months back, Willa told me that when she was seventeen, she'd been charged with involuntary manslaughter."

Winter snapped her chin up. "What?"

"She didn't give me many details, so I didn't think she was lying per se, but I felt like she was trying to make Rich look good. Like she generally did."

"You said something about manslaughter?"

"Yes. Willa and her boyfriend, Rich Benderell, were leaving a party. Or maybe headed to one. I think both. The sun was setting. She said she hadn't been drinking but he had been. She wasn't paying attention to the road and accidentally struck and killed a little girl who was walking her dog at a crosswalk. The girl died almost instantly."

Winter's lips parted, gears grinding in her mind. If Willa was sixteen at the time, that would've put the incident about eight years ago—right around the time Thatcher Templeton lost his daughter.

"Did she serve time?"

Dr. Poole shook her head. "Willa called 911 and confessed to the authorities. She pleaded guilty, but since she had no record and showed so much remorse, and she was a minor, she was given six months and probation with a fine. The day she came to talk to me was the anniversary of the girl's death."

The wheels turned furiously in Winter's head. "Did she tell you the girl's name?"

"No. Like I said, I got the feeling she wasn't quite telling me the whole truth." Dr. Poole's eyes were troubled. "Maybe not lying, but like she was leaving details out. I didn't press her, of course. I simply let her speak until she finished. I don't know if it's significant, but I thought you might want to know."

"You thought right." Winter nearly leaned in to hug the tiny woman but resisted. "Does Detective Davenport know about this?"

"No, I didn't remember it until after he left."

"Thank you. I'll be in touch." She needed to call Eve and Darnell and tell them everything she'd learned. She needed to get over to Dick Nichols Park too. There was no time to waste. She turned to go.

"One more thing," Dr. Poole called after her.

Winter stopped and clenched her fists, her feet on fire from how badly they itched to leave. She turned. "Yes?"

"After she told me that story, she asked me what I thought at the time was a non sequitur, but perhaps it was related."

Could you be a little wordier and more circuitous, please? I'm dying over here!

"Yes?"

"She asked me if I thought it was stupid for a person to sacrifice themselves for love."

The question hit hard enough to slow the wild beating of Winter's anxious heart. "What did you tell her?"

"I told her it wasn't stupid but that it was self-destructive. I encouraged her to act *out of* love instead of acting *for* it."

Winter smiled to herself even as tears pricked her eyes, thinking of the one for whom she would sacrifice anything. "I bet you're a pretty good therapist, huh?"

Dr. Poole sighed out a tired chuckle. "I really don't know anymore."

"If you think of anything...*an-y-thing*...call me right away. Even if it's three a.m. I mean it."

"I know you do." Setting her jaw, Dr. Poole straightened her pointy shoulders. "Good luck."

Normally, Winter didn't worry too much about luck, but playing Erik Saulson's games had left her feeling like a gambler at a roulette wheel. All it took was one bad turn, and she could lose everything.

She crossed her fingers as she left the office and jogged back to her SUV. Once inside, she made calls to Eve and Darnell. They both said they'd look into Willa York's case file. Maybe it held another piece to this very complicated puzzle.

Winter didn't know what she would find at Dick Nichols Park, but with what she'd just learned about Thatcher Templeton and Willa York, she might have finally gotten Saulson's number.

Unfortunately, the bubble she was trying to burst in her brain was as impermeable as ever. What in the world did Willa York and the park have to do with finding Noah? There had to be a connection. Saulson had sent Nancy York straight to Winter for that very reason. And the riddle *Where does TED go swimming?* was hiding under her husband's severed ring finger.

There had to be a connection.

27

Evening shadows stretched out long as Winter walked the many trails of the of the 152-acre park. She passed by play areas, picnic tables, a volleyball game. Heading vaguely for the pool, Winter kept the picture she'd taken of the painting open on her phone.

The best clue the painting gave was a knotted tree growing parallel to the ground that looked like it had fallen many years ago. The image showed its distinctive exposed roots, protruding from the dirt like a spider with knobby knees.

She circled the pool twice—found nothing—and returned to the trails.

Friendly dog walkers smiled as she passed. Kids played on the swings and the splash pad. Winter tried to ignore them. Somehow, the presence of children made every grim situation seem even grimmer.

Willa was dead. She felt it in her gut. Until she was sent to the park, she'd cherished the unlikely but tantalizing hope that Willa might still be alive. Now she knew she was looking for a body buried in this park.

This made sense to her—a busy park versus the middle of nowhere. This was all a game to him—the riskier, the better. Most likely, Willa died the same night she broke up with Rich and went to the bar with Chelsea. Maybe in her hotel room or somewhere nearby.

But whether finding Willa's decomposing body would lead her to a living and breathing Noah, she didn't know. She prayed more than anything that it would.

Winter would continue to play his games and solve his riddles and believe that it would take her to her husband. Erik Saulson would not break her.

Thatcher had been there that night, sitting in his apartment and eavesdropping on the fight next door. Gazing out the window to spy on Rich Benderell as he paced the parking lot. Chelsea and Missy had made it seem like Thatcher had an obsession with Willa—as if he were just another desperate creepy stalker who mistook his own sexual obsession for love.

But maybe that was simply their assumption. If Willa had been responsible for Thatcher's daughter's death, maybe he was obsessed with her for the same reason Erik Saulson was obsessed with Winter—to learn all the best ways to make her suffer.

She turned onto the Loop Trail, which took a long circle through the trees. Half an hour ticked by. She was nearly back to the parking lot when a gaggle of joggers approached from the other direction.

Stepping aside to let them pass, Winter caught a glimpse of a knotted tangle of roots.

She made a slow semicircle, looking at the trees and the trail from every angle until she found the exact match to the painting. After taking a picture, she picked up a random stick and drove it into the ground to mark the spot where the artist must've been sitting while painting. If Erik Saulson was still playing fair—and she suspected his own twisted rules were actually very important to him—then Willa was somewhere within this frame.

Leaving the path, Winter moved deeper into the trees, kicking branches and dead leaves and scanning the ground with her flashlight. She was looking for anything that didn't fit in—broken branches, crushed blossoms, and especially freshly turned dirt.

The sun was getting low on the horizon—another day coming to its end. Another day without Noah.

Fear brought gooseflesh to Winter's arms. "He's not here." Her voice came out so weak. "He's alive."

Noah was not buried in these woods. She felt it in her bones, just as sure as she felt Willa York *was* buried out here. Now maybe Noah's other shoe was buried with Willa, and in it was a clue as to his whereabouts. But that would be a dumb move, seeing as how Winter was sure Willa'd been gone for months, and Noah was just kidnapped.

No one would be crazy enough to dig up a grave to add some stupid riddle to it. That'd be like planting a flag atop a mound of dirt that said, *Body buried right here!*

Distracted, she caught the tip of her boot on a big branch of deadwood. She stumbled and had to catch herself on her knee against the cold, wet earth. Tiny flowers carpeted the forest floor, their colors all the same in the shadows, save one spot glowing faintly red—her powers calling her closer, assuring her that she was about to find what she was looking for.

She'd never been so grateful for her cursed, beautiful power.

Guided by the gentle glow, she came upon a soft bulge in the dirt. When she drew closer and shined her light on it, she saw new growth. A very faint dusting of plant life.

She rotated in a circle, looking at the earth.

The mound was circular, not the typical shape for a grave. But it was definitely big enough, and it had been dug sometime in the last few months. And from what she could tell from the little mound smack-dab in the middle of the bigger mound, someone had come back and messed with the area recently.

Saulson wasn't dumb. Whatever lay under the surface was intentional.

Flicking off her flashlight, Winter called Eve.

28

About twenty people had already gathered by the time I arrived at the park. It was a popular spot, and the body was found only a few dozen yards away from a busy trail. Police cars filled the lot, their lights whirling. The cops had strung yellow tape between the trees, and they'd set up superpowered halogen lamps to illuminate the darkening scene.

Inside the pool of light, Winter Black stood, her gaze fixed on the disturbed ground near the tree.

I was so angry, I thought my heart might explode. It was beating so hard in my chest, yet all my blood felt frozen.

How the hell had Winter Black found Willa York's body? I was already imagining myself slipping the bolt cutters around Erik's skinny-ass wrists and snapping his hands right off. *If this is his doing, he's dead.*

I needed answers. But I couldn't ask her. Trying to do so right now would do nothing but put a flashing sign over my head, letting everybody know what I had done.

I broke away from the crowd, jogged deep into the trees away from the scene, and yanked out my burner phone. My hands were sweaty and shaking, my breath so short, I worried I might pass out. I knew it wasn't smart to make the call when I was surrounded by law enforcement and so-called concerned citizens, but I had to. I needed to know the truth, and I needed to know it now.

Pressing the Call button, I waited for what felt like an eternity before the disgusting son of a bitch answered. "Yes?"

"What the hell did you do?"

He coughed out a little laugh. "Excuse me?"

I kept my voice low and deep, my eyes darting to make sure I was alone in my little corner of the woods. "You sold me out, you son of a bitch. I'll fucking kill you!"

"Calm down. Tell me what your issue is."

"Winter Black found Willa's body." I covered my mouth with my hand to try to muffle the sound. I was trembling. My head hurt. My fingers were numb.

"She finally solved my little riddle, hmm? I knew she would."

"Your riddle? I knew it. You told her! What game are you playing?"

"That's for me to know—"

"You better figure something out and fast. Because if you sell me out, I'm taking you down with me, *Erik Waller*."

After a quiet moment, he came back with a vengeance. "I know you're smart enough to assume her body would be uncovered at some point. You didn't leave anything on it that would lead back to you, did you?"

I rocked back and forth. "Spoken like somebody who knows dick-all about evidence collection. It's impossible to be one-hundred-percent sure you left no trace."

"Well, you're the expert on dead bodies."

"This is over, you hear me? I am through doing your dirty work. And if you do anything to try to expose me, I will turn you in so fast, you won't even have time to wonder what's going on before the cops are breaking down your door. Or should I say, breaking down your daddy's door?"

"Are you threatening me?" He sounded like he was speaking through clenched teeth. "I think you're forgetting something very important."

"I'm not forgetting shit. If you send me down, I'm taking you with me, asshole. Do you hear me?"

"You can't expose me without incriminating yourself."

A laugh that felt like it came from the edge of madness exploded from my lips. I had to slap a hand over my mouth to keep anyone back at the scene from hearing. "Tempt not a desperate man! I've fulfilled what I wanted to do. My daughter's killers got what they deserved."

"Boys like you don't last long in prison."

"Boys like me don't go to prison, Erik. Boys like me know how to keep records and do research. We write long emails, including every bit of evidence we've collected on you. Your name, your address, and every single phone call and text...I have it all recorded. I'll send them off right before I shoot myself in the head. You think I won't do it? You really want to play with me, Erik?"

"Oh, I think you know how much I love to play games." His tone was so smooth that I wanted to reach through the phone and smack some ripples into it. "In fact, I may need to pay a visit to 10617 Stone Haven Loop and play a game with the occupants there."

That was Marcy's address, my ex-wife. Erik always knew where to strike. She lived there with my son—the one she'd been pregnant with when she left me nearly nine years ago—along with her husband, who my son called *Dad*. "If you hurt them, I will break every bone in your body..."

"Would that make you feel better after I cut your wife into tiny pieces while making your son watch?"

He was bluffing. I was sure of it. The reason he used

people like me and Cybil Kerie was he didn't have the balls to do his own dirty work. So no way was he cutting anyone up.

The fact of the matter was, I had the advantage, because I wasn't trying to win anymore. The moment he gave me Rich Benderell's name, he'd let me off my leash. Now I was going to bite the shit out of him.

"I'll let Noah out," I said. "I'll tell him everything I know. Give him all my evidence. I'll set him loose, tell him where he can find you, and he will destroy you just like he did Carl Gardner."

He snarled, trying to speak through his angry stutter.

I knew bringing up Gardner would stick in his craw. I wasn't supposed to know about that, but he should've realized what he was getting himself into when he decided to start screwing with me. Did he seriously think I wouldn't research him?

He'd been so pissed about losing his computer expert. When he'd gotten the news, he'd stormed around the room like a toddler, looking for things to throw. I imagined he was destroying some personal property at this very moment. Erik had all the emotional maturity of a twelve-year-old.

"I have something you want," he said.

"What now, huh? You gonna try and tell me there were three people involved?" I laughed into his ear. "You've played all your cards, douche wad."

The phone vibrated from an incoming text message. I pulled it away from my ear and opened the picture he'd sent.

It was a cardboard box, the flaps open to show the contents. A baby doll, a stuffed rabbit, a well-loved pink blanket. A lock of golden hair from Quincy's first haircut.

My mind flashed back to the first time Erik Saulson had ever contacted me. He'd left a small cardboard package at my front door with a letter explaining that he could help me get justice against the person who'd killed my daughter. With it was a worn-out Barbie doll with wild curly hair and heart-shaped tattoos drawn all over her legs in permanent pink marker.

Her name was Sophia, and she'd been Quincy's favorite doll.

When I called Marcy to ask her about it, she'd accused me of breaking into her house and stealing it. Called me a monster and said she never wanted to speak to me again.

I'd already known I was a monster, and if I'd been a better husband and father, Marcy never would've left and Quincy would still be alive. I hadn't even argued with her.

The audacity of Erik, stealing the mementos of my daughter's brief life. How long had he been holding on to these treasures? I sure as hell wasn't going to let him keep them. It was an abomination. Whether I survived this ordeal or he exposed me in the end, Erik did not get to keep any piece of my daughter. Not one tiny piece.

Slowly, I lifted the phone to my ear. "You will give those back to me, or I'll—"

"It doesn't have to be like this, my friend." Erik sounded more confident now. "We're so close to the finish line. You don't have to get caught, and neither do I. You've got to trust me."

"Ha!"

"One last task, that's all. Just one last thing I need from you. Then I'll give you the box. I'll give you everything I have on you and cut you loose. You'll never hear from me again, I swear."

I looked at the picture again as a tear slid down my cheek. I had to get Quincy's belongings back. It was all that was left of her for those of us she'd left behind.

I knew Erik didn't have it in him to chop anybody up, but I didn't put it past him to con some other chump into doing it. In fact, I should've probably assumed I wasn't the only pathetic loser he was manipulating into doing his bidding right now.

"What do you want, Waller?" I would use his name as much as possible to make sure he didn't forget what I could do to him if he screwed me over again.

"You're at the scene right now, right?"

"Close enough."

"Good. Here's what I want you to do…"

I turned back toward the bright lights, scanning back and forth until I caught sight of Winter Black standing just inside the barrier of the crime scene tape. I couldn't see her face—just the silhouette of her body and long silky hair—but as she turned, I could've sworn she looked right at me.

29

Eve stepped up beside Detective Davenport and looked down at the freshly exhumed body of Willa York. The corpse was in an advanced state of decomposition—the M.E. on the scene estimated she had been dead for three months, give or take a week. Her body had been folded in half and then stuffed into a vintage-style suitcase made of thin wood and leather, already rotting from the moisture.

She wondered if the killer intentionally buried York right in the path of a sprinkler, where she was getting watered every day, speeding her decomposition. York was also within nine feet of a large eucalyptus tree, which was doing God's work in covering up the awful scent. Unfortunately, that meant nobody passing through the park had noticed a rotting smell, or if they had, it was fleeting before their senses were overtaken by nature's vapor rub.

Davenport cleared his throat and crouched near the body, his brown slacks stretching to reveal socks with orange flames on them à la Guy Fieri. "Do you know how Winter found the body?"

"Yes." Eve got down beside him and tilted her head. Willa

York was curled over herself like a fetus. "It looks like the killer dislocated her shoulders trying to get her in there."

When she blinked, she imagined a man standing over the suitcase, kicking the body with his foot to make it fit.

"Her nose is broken too. We'll have to get her out of there to confirm cause of death and get an ID."

"It's Willa York," Eve stated flatly.

"We can't know that officially." Darnell scowled. He had a wonderfully expressive, almost cartoonish face. She'd never once seen him smile, but she had a feeling it would light up a room just as easily as his scowl sent a cold tremor down her vertebrae. "You didn't answer my question."

"Yes, I did."

"Why are you being cagey?"

"Don't you know?" Eve leaned in for a better look at a tattoo on Willa's neck. A heart crossed with an infinity symbol and set atop a name. She could only read the last three letters, *-ich*. "Rich."

"What?"

Eve pointed at the tattoo. "Willa's ex-boyfriend, Rich Benderell."

His face morphed with disgust. "It should be illegal to get your partner's name tattooed onto your flesh."

"Oh, yeah? You got an ex-girlfriend crossed out on your butt?"

He gave her a death glare, but there was a whisper of amusement in his eyes. "Okay, clearly, you're going to make me ask again. How did Winter find the body?"

"That's a different question. Before you asked *if* I knew how she did it. Which I do. Am I gonna tell you how? That's a different answer."

"You're doing it on purpose now."

Eve set both hands on her knees to push back to her feet. She squinted against the harsh, unnatural lights and scanned for Winter. Those of the gathered crowd were pushing against one another, all eyes focused on her and Davenport—on the body.

Winter stood inside the yellow tape, but near the edge. Her focus was glued to her phone, and she was pacing in a small circle—up and down the bumper of a nearby cruiser. When Detective Lessner brushed past her, she didn't even look up.

Eve wasn't sure exactly how Winter had found Willa—only that she'd figured out that "TED" went swimming in a "Poole," and, somehow, that clue led her to the Blue Tree Wellness Center, which led her to a painting, which brought her here. And then, after that, it was all smoke and mirrors and visions and faint red glows.

Before Eve offered any official answers on her behalf, she needed to know what Winter had found on that wild-goose chase—other than Willa York, of course—and she really needed another pass at understanding exactly how she'd found it. But that was for another day. Locating Noah was the only thing on her mind at the moment.

"Fine. Be that way," Davenport said. "Winter needs to come to the station to give an official statement regardless."

"Let me talk to her first. She's nervous about sharing any information with the police right now. She doesn't know who she can trust. Neither do I."

His face soured like she'd just shoved a rotten lime between his teeth. "What proof do you have that there's a leak in my department?"

His department? Eve had to smile at that. She hadn't realized Davenport was out here keeping the city safe all by himself. She ought to get him a fruit basket or something.

Darnell once again treated her to his expressive scowl. "Isn't it possible this Erik Saulson guy is like every other kidnapper and is just trying to cover his own ass?"

She didn't even need to think about that one. "No."

"Why?"

Eve took a deep breath and sighed it out. Sometimes, having conversations with other investigators was so frustrating—like playing a game of *questions only* at an improv theater. "Eight years ago, Willa York struck a little girl with her car and killed her. Earlier today, I tried to pull that case from NCIC, and I wasn't able to."

Darnell gave her a strange look. "The file was corrupted, right?"

"Bingo. I couldn't get it to open. It was like somebody had scrambled it."

He shook his head. "Same thing happened to me, but I figured the system was glitching. Then all this came up."

Eve nodded.

"We have the paper files in our archives. I can pull it up the old-fashioned way."

"Maybe you can. I wouldn't be surprised if you run into problems, though."

Anger flashed in his eyes. "How could the print file be corrupted?"

She planted her hands on her hips. "I don't know, Darnell. Maybe someone accidentally on purpose spilled coffee on it. Or flushed it down a toilet."

Darnell pinched his lips together. "Maybe the leak is in the FBI. Did you ever think of that?"

"It very well could be. That doesn't really help Winter feel more trusting of others, though."

"She trusts you."

Eve lifted her gaze through the trees to glance at Winter again. "I hope so."

"There's something I need to show you."

Darnell took his phone out and showed her a picture of a

baggie with a series of numbers inside. It looked very familiar. Different numbers, same M.O. Saulson.

"Where was this?"

"It was buried about two feet above Willa York's body in this bag. Someone added it recently, within the last week or so, according to forensics. I took a snapshot to give to you and Winter before it got hauled off to evidence."

"Can you text that to me?"

Darnell sent Eve the photo. It was another string of numbers, fourteen digits long—*10211411251184.* Saulson had sent Winter a seven-digit number earlier in the week. They had to be connected. Eve had to get this to her.

"I'm gonna go talk with Winter." She stepped away from Darnell toward the back bumper of the cruiser. But when she looked around, Winter wasn't there anymore.

Eve jogged closer, thinking she might have simply stepped out of sight in her fervent pacing. She scanned the scene, darting between trees and cars, ignoring questions shouted at her by a few reporters mingled in with the growing crowd as she rushed past the yellow tape.

"Winter?" But calling for her was no use.

She was gone.

30

As Winter's gaze wandered over the scene, squinting in the powerful lights, she wondered who killed Willa York.

She didn't like Chelsea for the murder. But Chelsea could have been an unwilling pawn in the whole thing. Maybe she was a better actor than Winter gave her credit for.

Chelsea goes with Willa to a bar, follows her to the motel, calls Missy and Rich. Rich and Missy kill Willa, bury the body. Then Missy and Chelsea kill Rich because...why?

No.

Winter's thoughts tumbled off the edge of a cliff when her gaze wandered over the gathered crowd and then stopped dead on a familiar face—Thatcher Templeton from apartment 406.

He stood some distance from the tape, but with the positioning of the bright halogen lights, she easily saw his face even under the shadow of his baseball cap. Winter stared at him, every alarm bell in her head ringing. He shifted uncomfortably, like he could feel someone watching him. When his eyes locked on hers, they widened.

Winter dropped her phone into her back pocket and ducked under the tape. When she looked up again, she saw the back of his head retreating from the crowd. With all the requisite *Excuse me's*, she pushed her way through the crowd. When she came out the other side, she was blinded by a flash of light.

"Winter! Winter Black?" A woman flashed her camera at Winter. Little dots drifted through her vision. She shut her eyes tightly to try to recalibrate.

"Andrea Platter with crime tracker three-sixty dot com. You're the one who found the body, isn't that right? What led you to this spot? Have we uncovered another victim of The Prodigy?"

Winter was too distracted to be properly disgusted. "No comment."

She shouldered past the woman and through the crowd back to the paved walkway. Thatcher had a deceased daughter. As a mortician, he would know where to bury a body to hide it in plain sight, at least temporarily. And his obsession with Willa could've been misinterpreted by her roommates.

Streetlamps glowed like silver in the leaves above as Winter closed her eyes and listened for the distinct sound of quick shoes pounding pavement. Sneakers on asphalt.

She turned toward it and jogged down the path to the parking lot, breaking from the understory just in time to see a truck pulling away. A tall man in a baseball cap sat behind the wheel.

"Wait!" Winter called, hurrying into the lot, but he threw it in drive and peeled out, his back bumper making sparks when it hit a speed bump.

"Son of a bitch." Winter bolted to her SUV and got it moving. Cracking her knuckles, she made an educated guess and took the quickest route back to his apartment complex.

When she reached the glass double doors that led into the lobby, her finger hesitated over the call button for apartment 406. She pressed the one right next to it.

The intercom rang a few times before a voice crackled through. "Hello?"

"Chelsea? It's Winter Black. Can you let me in, please?"

"Uh. Missy isn't here, and I'm just about to get in the bath…"

"I need to speak with Thatcher right away."

"He's in 406."

Winter pinched the bridge of her nose. Chelsea's best defense against being implicated in the plot to kill Willa was that she was…Chelsea. "I know. I want to surprise him."

"Oh, my god. You think he's the one who kidnapped Willa?"

Winter bit her lip. "I can't answer that yet. Can you please buzz me in?"

"Okay, fine. Good luck."

The door buzzed and clicked. Winter threw it open and ran to the elevators, but waiting for the car was infuriating. Instead, she threw open the stairwell and ran up four flights, her boots clanging on the metal.

When she reached Thatcher's door, Winter balled a fist and knocked loud enough for everybody on the floor to hear.

Finding a suspect lurking around a crime scene was often a pretty good indicator that they were up to something. Her theory about Missy having killed Willa was rocky at best, and it wasn't leading her any closer to Noah. If Thatcher Templeton was behind all this—if anger over the death of his daughter drove him to Erik Saulson—he might have done anything to get revenge. That could include doing Erik's dirty work by kidnapping Noah and imprisoning him in his apartment.

"Thatcher?"

Bang, bang, bang.

"Open up. I need to speak with you. Now."

A chain rattled, and the door opened. He looked startled and red in the cheeks, like he'd been running and wasn't used to it. "Can I help you?"

Winter tilted her head subtly to peer through the gap under his arm into his apartment. She couldn't see much, save a massive picture of what looked like an alligator with wings hanging over his mantle.

"Why'd you run away?"

"Excuse me?"

"Don't play dumb. Dick Nichols Park."

He cleared his throat, took off his hat, and hung it on a hook by the door. "I was just listening to my police scanner and heard that a body was found. I wanted to go check it out."

"Why?"

He lifted one pointy shoulder. "Why do you care? There were tons of people there. Why are you here bothering me?"

"Because the other people there were just curious park goers and hikers. And you're the only person I saw in the crowd who has a personal connection to the victim."

His eyes widened to show a circle of white. "What? You don't mean that was Willa?"

Breath seethed out of Winter's nostrils. "I'm going to ask you one more time. What were you doing at the park tonight, and why did you run away from me?"

"I didn't run. I was just ready to leave. I didn't even see you."

He was lying. She knew it, and he knew she knew it. She was so sick of these stupid games.

He wriggled and squirmed, then let out a heavy sigh. "Are they sure it's Willa?"

The true answer to that question was of little

consequence to this conversation. Winter was sure, though. "Yes."

Templeton slumped, his shoulder hitting the doorjamb. Lifting onto her tiptoes, she caught a glimpse inside. His entire apartment was encircled by tall bookshelves stuffed to the gills. He even had one set up right behind him in the entry. A row of books, each bound with identical red leather covers, graced the shelves. *The Encyclopedia of Cryptids.*

She wrinkled her nose.

"Look," he moved to block her view, "you know the business I'm in. Death is kind of my bread and butter. And I..." He bit his lip and cast his gaze downward. "I like to keep track of any potentially mysterious cases."

"Why?"

"I work with the M.E.'s office all the time, and I'm often called to testify in court about things I find. I have to keep up with what's going on in the city."

It seemed a decent enough excuse, but he was still lying. Winter felt it in her bones. If he was Saulson's lackey—and Templeton was prime for Erik Saulson's particular brand of emotional manipulation—did he know who killed Willa? Or where Noah was?

Bleeding and frightened and waiting for her to come save him.

"Are we done?"

He went to close the door, but she stopped it with her boot. "Nope."

"What the hell are you doing?"

"If you cared about Willa like you said you did, then you'd be bending over backward to try to help."

Her words seemed to hit their target as his eyes darkened and his shoulders drooped. "Fine." Thatcher stepped aside, holding open the door with his body. "Do you want to come in?"

Winter slipped past him. If he was the killer, she could be putting herself in serious danger. She couldn't bring herself to care. For even a shred of a chance Noah was somewhere inside, she'd have crawled over broken glass to get to him.

"I need to ask you about your daughter."

His whole body tightened, upper lip curling. "Why?"

"It's related to Willa."

He blinked and lowered his brows, seeming genuinely confused.

"I'm following a lead, and the sooner I find the end of it, the sooner I can start chasing after something else. Please."

Thatcher sat on the edge of an oversized chair in the middle of the room. "I lost my daughter eight years ago. Nine this coming September."

"I'm very sorry for your loss."

"You don't know anything about my loss."

"How did it happen?"

He crossed and uncrossed his legs, looking as uncomfortable as a man with fire ants crawling in his pajamas. "We were driving home from dance class one night, me and Brittany, when a drunk driver jumped the median and slammed into our car going ninety miles per hour. I was driving. I tried to swerve, but there was nothing I could do."

A tiny thorn spiked in Winter's heart. "Please go on."

"The driver of the other car and his passenger were both killed on impact. Brittany and I were rushed to the hospital. I was in a coma for three weeks and had to go through a lot of physical therapy, but my daughter…" His voice choked, and he looked away. Little red splotches had formed on his cheeks, and mist coiled in his eyes. "She was pronounced dead on arrival."

That one thorn propagated into an entire bush, threatening to rip Winter apart. The timeline and outcome were similar, but otherwise the stories didn't line up.

"Are there any other painful memories you'd like me to share with you, Ms. Black?" He swiped his hand across his eyes. "I could tell you about the time my parents forgot me at a truck stop? Or maybe all the times I was bullied in high school?"

Winter shook her head slowly. "I'm sorry." She pressed a hand to her chest to try to hold her bleeding heart in place. "Thank you for sharing your story with me."

"It's not something most people know about me."

Winter took a slow breath. "My husband. He's been kidnapped. I think by the same person or by an associate of whoever killed Willa and Rich. I'm looking for him. And whoever has him, they're hurting him. They cut off one of his…" She bit down on her lip, hard enough to draw blood.

All the harshness melted from Thatcher Templeton's face in an instant.

To Winter's surprise, he reached out and put a gentle hand on her arm. She was even more surprised to find that she felt better disposed toward him, instead of reacting with an immediate need to knock his teeth down his throat, as she usually did when men touched her uninvited. Like he was just an aching soul and so was she, and they were seeing one another clearly for the very first time.

"I'm sorry I was angry." He let go of her. "Anything you need, I'll help. Of course I will."

"Thank you." Winter sniffed hard to hold back all the tears threatening to fall. Without another word, she slipped out of the apartment, and he closed and latched the door behind her.

Another dead end.

Tears sprang to her eyes like drops of hot rain splashing her face from above. Though she tried to keep them out, thoughts of Noah's severed finger torpedoed through her brain and tossed about her stomach. When Saulson—or whoever it was—cut off Noah's finger, had they cared for the wound properly? What if it got infected? He could go into shock or contract sepsis.

"Where are you, Noah?" she whispered to the elevator doors as they closed.

31

Winter saw it the second she emerged through the apartment complex doors. A white envelope on the hood of her SUV.

The only thing she knew for certain was that Templeton hadn't put it there. A person couldn't be in two places at once, last she checked.

Winter opened her door, popped the glove box, and put on some gloves before removing the envelope from her windshield.

She trembled with impatience and unceremoniously ripped it open. Before she read a word, she double- and triple-checked nothing else was inside.

Teeth clenched with rage, she read the letter.

Congratulations! You've reached the next level and are one step closer to the final boss battle.

Your mission, see husband again.

Status, you have collected all clues.

New Task, Time attack. Solve before 10 a.m. or husband gets KO'd forever.

Complete task to unlock New Mission—"Vengeance."

Ready player? GO!

The paper shook in her hands. Ten in the morning was fourteen hours away.

She turned the paper over far more times than necessary and held it up to the light to look for watermarks, more clues, anything. There was nothing. What the hell did he mean, she had everything she needed to find Noah? She didn't have anything!

Rage surged through Winter. Hissing to hold in the pain, she shoved the letter back up under her nose and read it again and again.

Status, you have collected all clues.

She didn't doubt it. Saulson had proven himself to be many things but not yet a liar. Now if only she could figure out what the hell he was talking about. But she sure as shit didn't feel as if she'd collected all the clues to find Noah.

She looked at her phone to see a string of texts from Eve. Her phone rang before she could read any of them.

"I just got off a call with Willa York's mom." Eve spoke at a fast clip. "She's heading in to provide a DNA sample so we can identify the body from Dick Nichols Park."

Clenching her teeth to stifle a sigh, Winter rubbed her temple. "Poor woman. Have they confirmed when she was killed?"

"The state of the body is looking consistent for her to have been killed on the night in question. I just got off the phone with Darnell. The manager at the motel where Willa stayed said she was only there one night and left in the morning by the time the cleaners came in. She never turned in her key card."

"She was dead by then." Winter kicked at the ground.

"Darnell said the manager couldn't think of anything suspicious. And they don't run surveillance. You know, the way seedy motels usually don't. With the place situated next to the highway, there're no other businesses around we can ask for theirs. So we don't know her movements after she left. But forensics found an acrylic nail that appeared to be ripped off."

"It's hers."

"Could be anyone's. Women pick those things off and discard them like toenail clippings. They'll compare the DNA, of course, and keep us posted."

"Do you know yet how Willa died? Is it consistent with what happened to Rich?"

"It looks like she was beaten around the face and neck with a blunt object and then manually strangled. Which is odd, because if she was killed in the motel room, there should've been blood. Unless we're dealing with somebody who knows all the best tricks for cleaning up a crime scene. In which case—"

"We're looking for someone in our line of work. A medical examiner, a forensic tech…a mortician." Winter craned her neck to look up at the apartment building. Had she misjudged Thatcher? She paced in little circles outside the entrance, waiting for somebody to come by and open it. If no one wandered by, she'd just ping Chelsea again.

"There was one thing, though. They found a waxy substance under Willa's fingernails. They sent it to the lab for testing. The M.E. thinks it might contain skin from our killer."

"His skin is waxy?"

"He theorized it might be lotion or some kind of skin cream."

The man with a burned wrist in the Insta photos flashed in her mind's eye. "There was a man at the bar with Willa and Chelsea with a burned wrist. Or maybe some kind of a nasty rash. So maybe if we find that burned wrist, we'll find our killer."

"Davenport said he'd pull the physical file of Willa's

manslaughter case from their archives and send it over today."

"You couldn't find it in the NCIC?"

"The file was corrupted and wouldn't pull. We both tried."

Eve sighed. "I'm getting the feeling that is not a coincidence."

"Coincidences don't exist."

"Sure they do. They're just always bad. And speaking of bad things…"

Winter's stomach dropped. Everything they were already discussing was about really bad, horrible things. "Is this about Noah?"

"Yes, and I've been hunting you down. You ran from the scene like you were on fire. There was a clue on top of Willa's bod—"

"Buried recently?" Winter clenched her fist.

"Yup, in the last week, according to Darnell. Encased in a plastic baggie. Another string of numbers. I sent you an image of it."

She stopped pacing and unclenched her fist. "So that's what Saulson meant when he said, 'Status, you have collected all clues.'"

"What's that now?"

"Meet me at my office. We need to compare notes, and time is running out."

"See you there."

Winter looked through Eve's text. There was the photo of the note sealed safely inside the baggie, bearing a string of fourteen digits. *10211411251184.*

She glanced heavenward and saw nothing but gray storm clouds bringing more rain.

The simple or obvious explanation to all this was that Erik Saulson killed Willa York. He needed to plant Cybil Kerie next to Dr. Poole in order to get Cybil to do dirty work for him. He used Cybil to get to Winter, and Cybil used the opportunity to frame Dr. Poole. Then he killed Cybil once she ratted him out.

Then he kidnapped Noah, and he decided to use Willa's grave as a place to leave a clue to Noah's whereabouts.

But this situation was neither simple nor obvious. Saulson didn't like to get his hands dirty. His M.O. was psychological and emotional manipulation. He had an accomplice—somebody doing all the manual labor while he sat back and congratulated himself on being the idea man.

Somebody with an axe to grind with Willa.

A man who needed to wear ointment on his skin. Possibly for red, scaly patches on his wrist.

Saulson could have an army of people working under him, for all she knew. How else did he always manage to stay one step ahead? And what was his endgame? To stalk her, torture her, destroy her morale?

Saulson said he'd given her everything she needed to find Noah. She just had to clear her mental cache and crunch the numbers.

"Numbers…" Getting into her SUV, she cranked the ignition.

These numbers were the only thing that didn't make sense yet, and that meant they were the key to the final puzzle.

The sun couldn't possibly rise fast enough, yet she wanted it to stay down forever. Noah had less than fourteen hours left.

32

At her office, Winter had cleared her desk with a swooping arm, knocking all her papers to the floor. Eve entered shortly thereafter, and they'd been working to crack Saulson's two numerical codes ever since.

That was over eleven hours ago, giving her only three hours to meet the maniac's deadline.

They were both slaphappy—and they looked it—but doing their best to stay focused. Eve had just returned from making her second coffee run, which was more about grabbing something for them to snack on. And by "them," Winter knew she meant her.

So Winter did her best to pick at a muffin. She peeked over her laptop at Eve. "Any luck on Willa's case?"

Eve stood and stretched. "I'm headed to PD right now. Davenport said he searched up and down for her physical file, but he has court again this morning. I'm gonna go look myself."

"How could the file just be missing? That doesn't make any sense."

"You know what doesn't make sense? That Nancy York could barely remember her daughter's case. Darnell said she didn't know the name of the little girl she hit. Didn't even remember it was a girl." Eve ran her hands through her hair. "Mom of the Year right there."

"Yeah, that was my impression when I met her. Well, that news just sucks on so many levels." Winter opened her word processor and hunted down the voice-to-text feature.

She dug into her cloud files, opened the voicemail she'd saved from Saulson, and let it play quietly, his words faithfully reproduced on the screen.

"He hinted we couldn't trust the police, right? And that was more than just a bluff."

Eve shook her head. "If he does have friends in the department, it'd have to be someone pretty high up to be able to disappear a damn murder case. Manslaughter. Whatever."

Winter barely registered her words. She'd spent the night trying everything to make sense of those damn numbers—reading them forward, backward, grouping them into threes like coordinates. When that didn't work, she plugged them into mapping tools, thinking they might represent grid locations or geographical data. She even ran them through apps designed to solve cipher puzzles, but the software spit out gibberish. Frustration clawed at her every time she hit a wall.

Eve's chosen trail to follow would lead them back to Erik's accomplice, but Winter wasn't sure if that would help them find Noah in time. She was focused on the two strings of numbers, as she had been all night. "Let me know as soon as you talk to Darnell, when you know anything more."

"Will do. Oh, I almost forgot. The M.E. called before I walked in earlier with the muffins. The ointment under Willa's nails has been identified as Triamcinolone."

"What?"

"It's a topical steroid for things like psoriasis or eczema. They're still working on extracting the skin flakes from the goop. She said once they isolate a viable sample, we're looking at three weeks for DNA, even with a rush."

Winter groaned. That would be too late to do them any good now. She pulled up images of psoriasis and eczema, comparing them to the arm in the Instagram photos of Willa York, ultimately concluding the rash looked more like eczema. The information churned in her brain. Eczema, the arm, eczema, the arm, over and over like a wash on spin cycle until the machine abruptly stopped. She jumped to her feet. "Lessner." The name exploded from her mouth.

"What?" Eve had almost shut the door behind her while Winter contemplated, but she leaned back inside.

Winter pushed away from the desk. "Lessner has a skin condition and wears long sleeves all day long, even in that weird beach photo on his desk."

"Oh, yeah, that one with his wife where he looks…what's the word?" Eve stepped back into the foyer and shut the door.

"Happy."

"Doesn't even look like him. Looks like his evil twin. No, he's the evil twin."

Winter started pacing and counting on her fingers. "He's a cop, higher up, he's got some skin condition, he's… dammit!" She slapped the print button, and the machine whirred, pushing out the transcripts she'd made of Erik Saulson's communications. "We have to call—"

"Ringing." Eve held out her phone to show she was one step ahead. "Darnell, hey, Eve and Winter here."

"Speaker." Winter motioned. "Put it on speaker."

Eve hit the button.

"Darnell, do you know anything about Lessner's medical condition?"

"His what?"

"Never mind." Winter shook her head, trying to focus. "That photo on his desk. Do you know anything about that?"

"You mean with his ex-wife?"

"Ex-wife?" Eve made a face like she just drank rotten milk. "What kind of freak keeps a photo of his ex-wife on his desk?"

"The kind that lost a child."

A chill ran down Winter's spine. "Lessner lost a child? Do you know how?"

She already knew how.

"Terrible car accident, girl was young. She was walking her dog and got hit. Happened a long time ago, though. What's this about?"

"Eight years?" Winter's heart was screaming at her to talk faster. "Did it happen eight years ago?"

"Yeah, Black, sounds about—"

"'You never know just who you'll be after the hammer falls.'" Lessner's words poured out of Winter.

"What the hell is she talking about, Taggart?"

"Lemme find out." Eve cocked her head. "What the hell are you talking about?"

It was so obvious now, Winter wanted to kick herself. "It's Lessner."

"What?"

"Willa killed Lessner's daughter. And Lessner killed her. And Rich." She thought back to her conversation with Lessner. The way he dodged questions and deflected and told lies. He'd seemed guilty to her then.

"Who killed Rich Benderell?" Darnell asked, his voice incredulous. "Lessner?"

"I bet Rich was in the car. Maybe he was even driving. And he let Willa take the fall." Winter clapped her hands together so hard, they stung. "That's why he couldn't break up with her."

Eve held up a hand. "Rewind a bit. You think Willa York killed Lessner's daughter?"

"A dirty cop, access to everything." Winter slammed her palm on the desk. "I think Rich was driving the car that killed Lessner's daughter. Willa took the fall. Lessner killed them both and corrupted her old file, lost it, whatever. Well, Erik Saulson probably corrupted Willa York's files for him."

"I need to put out a BOLO for Detective Harlan Lessner right away," Darnell said.

"Or, and call me crazy," Eve jumped in, "you could walk over to his desk and arrest him."

"I'm afraid Lessner's in the wind. Didn't show up for work this morning. Dammit, how the hell did I miss this?"

Before Winter could answer, the screen went black. She glanced at the clock.

7:17…

Fear crawled over her skin. Taking a step back, she reviewed all they'd done during the night. They'd explored countless wrong turns. In addition to the cipher apps, they'd used cryptographic equations and even statistical analysis. Mapping coordinates had failed, even after grouping the numbers into random patterns.

Nothing fit.

Saulson's riddle was maddeningly resistant to logic.

What was she missing?

For the next hour, while the Austin PD started a manhunt for Detective Harlan Lessner and Eve went to the Bureau to get Falkner up to speed, Winter zeroed back in on decoding Saulson's number puzzle.

She read the numbers out loud—as single digits, as

groups of two, as groups of three. Then she read them again in reverse. Snatching up two sticky notes, she wrote them down, putting them side by side one way, then the other—2591414, 10211411251184.

She tried adding them all together, multiplying, finding the mean, median, and mode.

A glance at the clock showed 8:21—one hour and thirty-nine minutes remained before she lost Saulson's game.

And Noah.

Her body shook with frustration, and her brain ached. She was physically ill, not just because of the time crunch, but because she'd been playing with these two sets of numbers all night long. She was damn near losing her mind.

Winter grabbed her hair and yanked. "Okay, okay, okay. Something he says. Numbers." She stepped to the window into a slant of morning light, closed her eyes, and forced herself to take a deep slow breath. "Clear your cache. I am calm. I am in control. I am unstoppable." With a growl, she arched her back, twisted in both directions, and turned to her desk with a renewed sense of vigor.

Don't read. Just see.

Though the instructions her mind provided didn't make sense, she took a step back and gazed at the numbers again. Instead of reading them as numbers, she simply followed the lines and curves on the paper. Not processing, just letting the patterns sink in.

"What could data like that be referring to?"

Winter's brain flashed back to the last math class she'd taken in college—statistics. Nothing. Then she recited the numbers out loud again, one by one. Then two by two.

"Fuck!" She was so sick of Saulson and his childish games. He was a damn child, an evil baby. And that's when it hit her.

He was, in fact, a child. This was a kid's game. Not some ancient Egyptian code or coordinates.

The numbers were letters that spelled two words.

2591414. That meant 2 was either the letter *B* or the number 25 was the letter *W*. It had to be *W*, because the number 59 did not line up with any letter in the twenty-six-letter English alphabet. So the next number, 9, aligned with the letter *I*. The number 14 aligned with the letter *N*, and there were two of those.

Winn.

Second word was hidden in the sequence 10211411251184.

It started with a 10, which was the letter *J*, and the next letter could not be 2, because that was the letter *B*, so it had to be 21, which was the letter *U*. In no time, Winter had spelled the second word—*junkyard.*

Winn Junkyard.

Her fingers were numb on the keys, fumbling and making mistakes as she typed *Winn Junkyard* into her GPS.

Just outside of Austin, about a mile from Walnut Creek.

Could Saulson really have just handed Noah's location over to her on a plate? Why in hell would he do that?

Unless he was setting her up to find something horrible…

Winter balled her fists, trying to force back the dread attempting to overtake her.

No way this wasn't a trap. Unless Saulson was so committed to the idea of gaming that he'd leave open a way for her to win? Could such a monstrous human actually have a sense of sportsmanship?

Winter laughed at herself—a stranger's voice coming from her own throat. "Of course he would. His ego forced him to. If he didn't offer any chances for me to beat him, then how could he gloat over it if I lose?"

But he'd underestimated her, time and again. She wouldn't lose. She wasn't afraid of his traps or his threats.

This was not her first rodeo, not her first time playing chess with an overconfident psychopath.

Winter snatched up her keys and ran out the door to her Pilot. She would find Noah and get him back. And then she'd hunt down Erik Saulson and show him what happened to anyone who dared to challenge her to a game of life and death.

33

Winter texted Eve.

Noah's at Winn Junkyard. Meet me there.

But she couldn't wait for her. It was already 9:18, and Saulson had given her 'til ten. Forty-eight minutes. She got on the highway and put the pedal to the floor, even driving on the shoulder to get past road construction and not giving a damn who flipped her off for doing it. When she hit a bit of open road outside the city, she pushed her Pilot up past one hundred, following the directions her phone gave her to Walnut Creek.

9:41.

After taking an off-ramp, she slowed and scanned the area. Flat and marshy, dotted by short trees and thick bushes. She came upon a wreckage yard of abandoned vehicles—some half crushed, some up on blocks with their tires missing, others stripped down to the chassis. Winter parked right in front of the gate and drew her weapon before stepping out.

Saulson could be somewhere on the lot, watching and waiting. He and his cronies might be hiding in one of the cars or lurking behind the bushes. For all she knew, he had guns pointed at her right at that moment, and the only thing keeping her alive was that he wanted it that way.

Then again, it would seem kind of pointless to go through everything they had for him to just shoot her in the back. Erik Saulson had a flair for the dramatic. In a way, she was thankful for that particular flaw of his. It was the reason she still lived.

The dull red glow of something her brain needed her to see caught her eye—a vehicle near the very back of the lot. Winter zeroed in on it and broke into a run, hopping over scraps of twisted metal and snaking through stacks of cars.

At last, she got a clear view of the glowing object—an old RV propped up on cinderblocks, its windows shaded.

Noah was in there. She knew it.

Her heart leaped, and a scraping, shrieking cry escaped her lips. Winter reached the RV and slammed against the door. She yanked the handle.

Locked.

Anger and frustration screamed out of her, fueling her muscles when she planted her back foot and kicked the lock. The thin metal bent. She kicked it again and again, putting every ounce of strength she had into it. The lock buckled. She hauled the door open.

Winter rushed inside. "Noah?"

Dappled light flowed over her. She had to squint and wait for her eyes to adjust before they could penetrate the darkness. The first thing she noticed was a sharp green glow in one corner before her gaze landed on what her heart longed to find.

He was all the way at the end of the RV, strapped down to the bed, arms and legs spread wide. His eyes were closed. He wasn't moving.

Emotion crashed through Winter, raw and brutal,

stealing her breath and nearly doubling her over. A strangled sob clawed its way out of her throat as she stumbled to his side, falling to her knees beside him. She hovered her trembling hands over his face, terrified to touch, terrified of what she might find.

"Noah..." Her voice broke on his name. She pressed her fingers to his cheek and chest. His skin was cold and clammy, but warm breath from his nose brushed faintly against her fingertips. She pressed her ear to his chest, desperate for confirmation, and there it was—a heartbeat. Slow, but steady.

Relief hit her like a tidal wave, and her entire body shook with the knowledge that he was alive. Now she just needed to make sure he stayed that way.

His skin was a sickly yellowish white, streaked with blood and sweat, and the putrid smell of vomit hung thick in the air. Panic clawed at the edges of her mind, but she shoved it down. Her tears threatened to overwhelm her, but she forced them back, inhaling sharply. She didn't have time to break.

"Noah, I'm here." Leather straps on his ankles. She cut those with her pocketknife, and another on his left arm—the one that was wrapped in black, blood-soaked gauze and smelled like rotted meat. Winter held back a gag. She crawled across the bed and reached over Noah to free his right hand.

Instead of a leather band, she touched metal. Handcuffs. One end was looped around his wrist, the other end secured to the RV's steel frame through a broken panel.

Though she'd fought an oncoming PTSD flashback, a memory cut out her vision for a split second. *Her arm handcuffed to a metal bar. An RV filled with screaming and crying. The snap of a neck breaking under her hands—*

Rage and panic flared so bright, she couldn't see straight even as her vision returned.

There was no way Saulson had sent Winter to an RV by accident. He was trying to freak her out, get her to lose focus. He knew too much about her history, about Justin's history.

Fuck this guy.

She tore herself up from the mattress and glanced around the RV. The green glow at the foot of the bed caught her attention again.

On closer inspection, she found a metal cylinder, like a large section of pipe, had been soldered to the floor. The green glow came from the screen of a cell phone duct-taped to the outside. It read *15:01* and was counting backward.

14:59, 14:58...

A countdown.

A surge of prickly ice rushed through Winter's brain and body as the full reality of Saulson's puzzle crashed over her. It was a pipe bomb. Chained to her husband. Set to go off in fourteen minutes and thirty-four seconds.

14:33, 14:32...

Winter rushed back to Noah and cupped his face in her hands. "Noah? Baby? You gotta wake up. Please!"

She slapped him lightly, but his head just slumped to the side. She didn't know if he was drugged or in shock, but it made no difference. He wasn't going to wake up. She had to drag him out.

In a panic, she grabbed the steel bar securing the cuffs and yanked with all her strength. Her muscles screamed in pain, but the bar didn't budge.

Yanking the handcuffs around her wrist, trying to pull the grab bar out of the—

Drawing herself back up, she glanced at the flickering green numbers.

12:48...

Winter screamed and threw her arms in the air. Turning in a circle, she searched for anything that would help.

She noticed a little white envelope on the opposite side of the bed near the window. A tiny piece of clear tape wiggled on the blinds above it. Another fucking envelope Saulson had left for her to find.

She snatched the envelope with numb fingers and unfolded the scrap of paper inside.

The weary taskmaster rolls. The carriage holds the key.

"Another fucking riddle!" In wild anger, she grabbed a big wooden cutting board from the tiny kitchen counter and threw it so hard, it broke through a window. She looked at the time.

11:32...

"Okay, okay, okay. Think." She pressed both hands over her face in a vain attempt to shield her brain. "Word games. Riddles. He gave you the answer."

On instinct, she snatched her phone out of her pocket and called the only person who could help.

Eve answered on the first ring. "I'm ten minutes out."

"I found Noah. He's handcuffed. There's a bomb. And Saulson left another fucking riddle!"

Eve said nothing for about ten precious seconds. "I just shot Falkner a text to rally the bomb squad and sent him the location." Voices chattered in the background. "Okay, he responded. He's on it. Now give me the riddle."

"'The weary taskmaster rolls. The carriage holds the key.'"

"The key to the cuffs. Okay. And you're the weary taskmaster."

"Eleven minutes, Eve!"

"Where can you roll? Is there a carriage around?"

"It's a wreckage yard. Noah's in an RV."

"So yes. Lots of carriages to roll under."

"The undercarriage!" Winter dropped the phone and raced out the door, falling to her belly in the dirt and rolling under the RV. She searched the ground and the twists of metal beneath the camper.

Nothing.

Winter rolled back out and slapped open the door of the RV to scrape up her phone. "It's not there!"

"Shit. Okay. Carriage is a synonym for cab. Cab means the front of the vehicle. Maybe under the seats?"

She hit speaker and shoved the phone in her back pocket. Stumbling to the cab, she ripped up the floor mats. Her tattered fingernails tore at the trash, fumbled under the seats.

"Nothing!" Winter looked back at Noah and the timer.

5:12, 5:11...

How had she lost so much time?

"There has to be more to the weary taskmaster part," Eve gasped through sharp breaths. "Taskmaster. That sounds so familiar to me. Something to do with cars…"

"Weary. I'm weary! I'm weary as fuck. And tired too."

Her head snapped up and, at the same time, they both shouted, "Tires!"

Winter all but fell out of the door onto the ground under the carriage's front tires, where she saw the brand name *Taskmaster* stamped on the rubber. She shoved her fingers under, not caring that it tore at her nails, and screamed in joy when she touched cold metal and pulled up a tiny silver key.

She raced back inside and dropped beside Noah. "I'm gonna get you out of here."

She grabbed the cuffs on his wrists. Her fingers shook, but through sheer force of will, she got the key in the lock. Mercifully, the key turned, and the cuffs popped open. She pulled Noah's wrist free.

3:11...

"Noah, please! You have to wake up!" She tried to sit him up, but he was so heavy. Fresh panic gripped her as she wondered if she would be strong enough to get him out.

"No!" Winter snatched his arm and yanked hard as if on a lever, positioning him with his head toward her. Then she looped her arms under his and dragged him onto the floor with a hard thud. Her muscles stretched and stung with pain, but she pulled and pulled, dragging all two hundred and forty pounds of the man she loved down the narrow aisle of the RV.

After kicking the door all the way open, she backed out down the stairs, dragging Noah behind her. Her foot slipped on the last step, and she stumbled back, twisting her ankle.

Her backside hit the hard earth. Inside the RV, a loud beep sounded.

Gathering her strength, she forced herself back to her feet and ignored the scream of her ankle. She snatched Noah by his shins, one in each hand, and dragged him behind her like a work horse plowing a field. One foot in front of the other, as strong and quick as she could muster. Sweat coated her forehead, dripping into her eyes.

One foot in front of the other.

Get to safety. Get as far away as you can.

The beeping intensified, quickening. She pulled Noah behind a ripped-up Oldsmobile. Falling to her knees, she covered his head with her body and clamped her hands over her ears as the final beep sounded.

A beat of silence was followed by a shattering boom that shook the very air. The flash of fire, the smell of gasoline. And then came the crash.

Winter waited a few moments before sitting up and peeking over the hood of the broken-down car that had protected her. Fire streamed through every shattered window of the RV, and the back door had blown out. If she had arrived even a minute later, Noah would still be in there.

Her knees went weak, and she collapsed over her

husband. Again, she touched his neck, his chest, his lips, making sure he was still alive. That he was real.

As grateful and relieved as she felt, anger tightened her jaw and clenched her teeth. She had never in her life wanted to hurt someone the way she wanted to hurt Erik Saulson. In the distance, a siren caught her ear, slowly drawing closer.

Eve.

"The police are on their way, Erik!" she screamed at the empty lot, knowing he was there somewhere, whether in person or watching through a camera. She snatched her gun back out of its holster and pressed her back against Noah, lying over him like a shield. "You better pray they catch you before I do!"

34

After flashing her badge at the hospital security desk, Eve took the elevator to the fourth floor, where Noah was being looked after. She hadn't spoken to Winter since this morning, when she'd arrived on the scene to find her crouched over her husband with a pointed gun while snarling like a mother tiger protecting her cub. He was alive.

Eve had almost fallen to her knees in that moment. She'd never said it out loud, but with every passing minute he was missing, a small piece of her hope had slipped away. She'd called an ambulance and had Winter and Noah taken back to the city while she stuck around to examine the scene.

The door to Noah's hospital room hung ajar by a few inches.

Eve paused to knock before stepping inside. Winter sat in a chair close by his side, his hand gripped tightly in hers. She looked like absolute death. Her black hair was wild, dusted with brown dirt, and inexplicably damp. Her clothes were filthy and wrinkled. When she looked up, she smiled, but the gray bags below her eyes contradicted the happy expression.

Eve imagined she didn't look much better. They'd both

been up all night solving the mystery of Noah's whereabouts, and neither of them had had a second to even splash water on their faces.

"Hey," Winter rasped.

"Hey." Eve stepped in, her rubber soles squeaking on the linoleum. Gradually, her gaze wandered to Noah. He was covered in scratches and bruises, with gauze wrapped around his left hand and over his head.

"He has a concussion," Winter answered before Eve had a chance to ask. "Four broken ribs, a dislocated shoulder, and his finger." She lifted her gaze. "You said you'd speak to the M.E. about preserving it…?"

Eve sighed through tight teeth. "I'm sorry. Too much time had already passed by the time you even got the finger. There was nothing anybody could've done."

Winter's eyes misted over, and she looked down at her husband, squeezing his good hand tighter with both of hers.

Eve stepped closer and touched Winter's trembling shoulder. "Has he woken up?"

"Yes, briefly." She gave a quick smile, this one still tired but genuine. "A few times, but he's really out of it. The doctors said he was given a lot of different drugs to knock him out. They say we just have to wait for his system to clear." She stroked the back of his hand. "His dog tags are missing. Did anybody find them?"

"I don't know. I'll ask." Eve dragged another chair over near the bed and sat down next to Winter.

"Have they found Lessner?"

"Nope. But they turned up Willa York's car in the junkyard. Good place for Lessner to hide it. Darnell is on his way to get a statement from Noah, if he's able. And I got a security detail on your grandparents' house. It's temporary, but—"

Without warning, Winter snatched Eve in her arms and hugged her tight. "Thank you."

Eve's heart swelled up so much that it hurt. Hot tears, which she'd been fighting ever since she rolled up on the scene at the burning RV, spilled from her eyes. She hugged her back, gently brushing down her rat's nest.

"Now I understand why Noah was always so distracted at work." Sniffling, Eve wiped back a tear and pulled away. "Being your husband is a full-time job."

Winter snorted, her eyes downcast.

"And my job's not over yet. But why don't you go stretch your legs, grab a bite? I'm gonna jaw at your man, if he'll let me."

Winter rose to unsteady feet. Then she leaned down and kissed Noah's forehead. "I'll be back soon, babe."

Turning her attention to Noah, Eve snatched up a pencil and pad of stationery from the nurse's desk.

"Hey." Eve grabbed Noah's shoulder and shook gently. He groaned and mumbled, his eyelids fluttering. "Are you there, big guy?"

Noah smacked his lips a few times, and his eyes finally opened all the way as he slowly focused on her. "Eve?"

"Hey, buddy. How's it going?"

He gave a little cough and winced in pain. "Where's Winter?"

"Just grabbing some food. Poor thing's been starving herself."

Noah closed his eyes, seemingly reassured, and let his head fall back on the pillow.

Eve grabbed his shoulder and shook him again. "Who did this to you? Was it Erik Saulson?"

"Erik?" He blinked a few times, ending up back with his eyes closed. "No. He was too fat."

"Really? Was he tall? Short?"

"Short but stocky. Like a gorilla. He cut my finger off, Eve. Off."

"I know."

A light knock came on the door, and a portly nurse in purple scrubs walked in. "Hi. Just coming in to top off your pain killers."

"Thank you. I like you very much." Noah's words slurred together.

The nurse smiled and stepped over to the IV, where she stabbed a syringe full of medicine into the port. It flowed through the saline, clouding the liquid in the plastic tube that ran into the vein on Noah's uninjured hand.

"Greasy," Noah said.

Both the nurse and Eve cocked their heads at him. "What?"

"The man. The short, fat man. He smelled greasy."

Eve scooched closer in her chair. "What do you mean by that? Greasy can mean so many things."

"Spicy." His words faded into each other as sleep reclaimed him. "Pepper."

"Was he cooking? I don't understand."

"Fried chicken…" Noah's head slumped into his pillow. He made a few more ill-conceived attempts at speech before he began snoring loudly. But Eve had the verification she needed. He'd just described Lessner to a T.

❆

Winter freshened up in the restroom, splashing water on her face and running her fingers through her hair. She was halfway to the elevators when she remembered—food. Eve would bitch her out if she came back empty-handed. She went to the cafeteria and grabbed a couple of simple turkey sandwiches, one for her new friend...or whatever Eve was to her now. More like family.

She stepped onto the empty elevator and pressed the button for Noah's floor. She leaned back on the wall, but every muscle in her body was on a hair trigger, and her ankle still smarted. The words of Erik Saulson's last letter ran through her brain on an endless loop, like a song on repeat.

He hadn't said she had until that morning to *find* Noah or to *rescue* him. He said she had until then to see him again. And if she *succeeded*, she'd unlock a new mission.

A mission he called *"Vengeance."*

Panic took hold very slowly, only hitting her heart as the elevator climbed upward. In Saulson's game, Noah was dead before the final battle. What she'd been fighting for all this time was just a chance to say goodbye.

Winter sprang away from the wall, but the elevator rose with agonizing slowness. Saulson still wanted Noah dead. And Lessner, his lapdog, had already signed on to pull the trigger.

35

"You got the package I dropped for you?" Erik gurgled in my ear.

I glared at the paper box and the coveralls he'd left on my passenger seat, my knuckles white on the wheel even though the car was still in park. The video Erik had just sent me was on replay in my head. It showed me in broad daylight stepping out of my car, suiting myself up in Tyvek, and entering the RV with the bolt cutters in hand.

A minute later, Noah's scream cracked the sound barrier, after which I reappeared in frame, blood spattered on my coveralls and dripping from the bolt cutters.

The son of a bitch had me over a barrel. Why hadn't I checked for cameras at the wreckage yard? I looked for them inside the RV…but what the hell was I thinking? I sure as hell wasn't thinking like a cop. All the immoral lawbreaking aside, they ought to take my badge away on grounds of stupidity alone.

I clenched my jaw hard. "If you squeal on me, I'll squeal on you, Waller. I know your name. I know who your parents are."

"Squeal all you want, pig!" A high-pitched, manic laugh rang through the phone. "I'm not even a person! I'm a ghost in a machine. Shit, I'll tell Winter my real name myself. In fact, that's exactly what I'm gonna do. Right after you kill her husband."

"You're bluffing." I so wanted that to be true, but the black tarry lump in my stomach knew better. Erik and I had been playing chicken long enough that we both knew who was going to veer off the path first.

"Do you know what happens to cops in prison, pig? Especially a homicide detective. And didn't you work vice for a while?" His voice dropped to a smooth singsong. "You'll be so popular. Entire gangs will be lining up to fuck you up."

I rocked back and forth in frustration. He wasn't wrong, but that wasn't what I was thinking about. I had to live long enough to hunt him down and kill the creepy little shit stain myself. Yes, he'd helped me get revenge on Willa York and Rich Benderell for killing my little girl, my sunshine. But he did it by using her memory like a prop in one of his damn games. It was unforgivable, and I was going to make him pay.

The son of a bitch filmed me doing his dirty work to blackmail me into doing more.

"Put on the outfit I left for you, bitch," Erik seethed. "The janitor's entrance is open. And that badge works."

"How did you—"

"When will you get it through your head that I can do whatever the fuck I want?"

I blinked in the harsh light of day, gazing up at the hospital and wondering if that might actually be true. I already had his damn costume on.

"You have to get this done quickly and get out of town," Erik continued. "I'll send you the coordinates to a safe spot where I left the box full of your daughter's things."

"I can't go in there. They'll catch me."

"If you don't go in there, I'm sending this video directly to Darnell Davenport's email. I'll tell him where to find everything else he needs. And then everybody will know the extent of what you did. Do you think Marcy will be proud of you then?"

Growling in frustration, I punched the dash. "I'm going to kill you!"

"Winter got to see her husband again." Erik's voice was so thick with saliva, he sounded ravenous. "But she always misunderstood the mission. And sometimes an NPC needs to be sacrificed to keep the plot moving."

NPC. I fought to place the unfamiliar term.

Then it clicked. Non-player character. The kind of background figure you barely noticed in a game. Expendable. Someone who didn't matter except to push the story forward.

My stomach churned. "You're out of your damn mind."

Erik's laugh crackled through the line. "Sacrifices make for better drama, don't you think? That little blond bitch is in there…Agent Eve Taggart. Take her out too." He said it as casually as ordering a side of fries. "Winter relies on her too much. She's an obstacle, and I need the player isolated. I need her with no connections, no one to trust, and nowhere to run."

"Taggart is not part of the deal."

"I'm not making deals with you anymore. I own you, bitch. I own you! I want them dead, do you hear me? You have ten minutes." He hung up

Rage flooded through me, shaking my bones. I balled a fist and punched my dashboard over and over until my knuckles stung.

When I was out of breath, I opened my glove compartment and cleaned the pinpricks of blood from my hands with sanitizing wipes that stung worse than bees. Jaw clenched so hard my teeth hurt, I put on gloves and snatched up the badge.

"Fine, Erik!" I got out of the car and slapped the door closed. He thought I cared about going to prison. He thought I cared about any of his stupid threats.

He thought wrong.

I'd go through with this. Finish off Noah and even Special Agent Taggart if I had to, but only so I could get a step closer to Erik. He'd stolen every last thing from me—my memories and my ex-wife. The last of Quincy. The thought of his disgusting hands touching my sunshine's blanket or her dolls. Of him looking at her picture…

I even had on the stupid wig and glasses he'd left for me. For good measure, I put on a surgical mask. The jumpsuit was miserable, tearing at the upraised welts on my arms and the back of my neck. Ten minutes, he'd said. I'd be in and out of there.

Marching up to the back door of the hospital, I used the badge to get in. Erik had also sent detailed instructions of which elevator to take and which halls to walk down. I felt like I was executing a coordinated maneuver with whatever worm he had on the hook at the hospital who was facilitating all this.

It should not have been this easy to sneak inside, even with a wig and working badge. Someone else was covering for me. How many people was he torturing and blackmailing and manipulating? Dozens? More?

I slammed my fist into the big button to call the freight elevator and waited. When it creaked its way to my floor, I stepped inside and rode it up. I hated Erik, but I found myself hating Marcy, too, for not protecting Quincy's things better, keeping them in a carboard box stuffed in her attic like they didn't matter.

On some level, I'd always thought Marcy and I were in

the same boat, grieving our baby girl. But that wasn't true at all. While I was fighting and sacrificing myself in the name of her memory, all that heartless bitch wanted to do was forget.

The elevator doors slid open, and I stepped into the hall. Ten minutes, he'd said. Eight and a half now. A nurse rushed down the hall, and I slipped into an empty patient room to hide until she passed. In the darkness, I took out my gun and checked it over. Fully loaded, clean, ready to fire.

I shouldn't use the gun. I'd have to do this swiftly and silently and then get the hell out of Austin and to the safe house as quickly as possible.

My jaw trembled. I didn't want to do this, but what choice did I have? I'd crossed the thin blue line the night I killed Willa York, and especially when I'd kidnapped and mutilated Noah Dalton.

I still felt guilty about that. I didn't want to hurt him. Or his old partner, Eve Taggart. Or Winter Black for that matter. But I didn't have a choice. I had to get Quincy's box back. Holding those treasures in my hands was the closest I could ever come to holding my daughter again.

And to get my little girl's things back, Eve and Noah had to die. Winter had to suffer.

Speed and surprise were my allies. They weren't expecting me, and it would all be over so fast. They'd never know what hit them.

Holstering my gun in the back of my belt, I slipped into the empty hallway and hurried to Noah's room. The door hung slightly ajar—no cops stationed out front. That meant they'd be inside the room with him. At least Taggart.

My heart hummed as I nudged the door open and slid inside. Noah was the only patient in a double room. He lay unconscious and broken. Monitors and machines beeped to his right next to Agent Taggart, whose back was to the door.

She turned slowly, and her blue eyes snapped to mine. "We don't need the room serviced right now, thank you."

I didn't move.

She took a step toward me, narrowing her gaze, as if that would help her see behind my glasses. Her nostrils flared as she took a deep inhale, and then her eyes widened. "Fried chicken..." As she glanced at Noah, then back at me, her body stiffened.

She knows.

My hand instinctively went to my gun but stopped short. The sharp bang of a gunshot would echo through the entire hospital, sending nurses, doctors, and security flooding in before I could finish the job. Stealth was key. If I made a noise like that, it wouldn't just blow my cover—it would end this whole thing before it even started.

Eve Taggart was a tiny woman—and I had a good one hundred pounds on her.

This would be easy.

But before I could move, Taggart's hand went to her own gun. "Lessner, you're under arrest for the murd—"

I barreled into her, not letting her finish. She tried to call out for help and kicked with her legs to trip me, but I was too big, my legs too strong. I fell on top of her, knocking a chair aside, and I managed to cover her mouth.

I had her pinned, so I wrapped my other hand around her neck.

She had to die because Erik had to die. And Erik *had* to die.

I squeezed harder. She tried to get her legs up around me, to get her hands under mine—every trick they taught to help an agent save themselves. But I knew all the same tricks. And I was so much stronger.

Her eyes bulged. She batted my glasses off my face, and the wig fell too. But she was losing oxygen, losing the fight. I didn't need to cover her mouth anymore, so I moved my other hand to her neck to get this over with.

She scratched the skin on my hands, puncturing the gloves, and creating bloody streaks where she'd shredded the skin. I steeled myself. I shook her, striking the back of her head hard on the tile—again and again until blood trickled and began to pool.

At last, her strength slipped away, but I squeezed harder and harder, my mouth foaming. For Quincy, I told myself. This was all for Quincy. I had to make sure she was dead.

Noah moaned from the bed.

Panicked, I dropped Eve and rose to my feet.

His eyes were half opened, mouth mumbling. Too awake. I had to finish him off quickly. But when I searched the room for a makeshift weapon, nothing caught my eye.

Screw it. I reached for my gun. Using a pillow to muffle the sound, all I needed was one quick shot right in the brain, then I'd run. They'd never know which way I'd gone until it was too late.

36

With her heart in her throat, Winter burst through the door to Noah's hospital room and froze.

Eve lay on the floor at her feet, in front of all his machines, a pool of blood circling her head. She wasn't moving.

Lessner stood beside Noah's bed, gun in hand, pointed at Noah's skull.

Winter stumbled to a halt at the side of the bed. "Wait! You don't have to do this."

His head snapped back as he looked at her, but his gun held steady. The sleeve of his janitor's coveralls pulled back from his extended arm, where a crusty red blotch of dried-up skin crawled from his wrist to his elbow. "You're wrong. I have to! I don't have choice."

"I understand why you did what you did to Willa." Winter swallowed the lump in her throat. "What she did to Quincy."

His face tightened painfully, eyes wild. "Don't say her name."

Winter held her hands up. "I'm sorry."

"And Benderell killed my daughter. While flying high on

mushrooms. He killed my little girl and let his girlfriend take the blame!" Lessner's voice choked.

She couldn't tell if those were tears in his perpetually watery eyes, but she'd never heard his voice sound like that. Never seen him so overcome with emotion.

"So you killed him too."

"Yes." Lessner sniffed hard, the tendons in his neck bulging. The tip of the cold barrel rested against Noah's temple. "And I'd do it again! He deserved it, and so did she for covering it up, for letting him drive in the first place."

"I understand, okay? I do. But Noah didn't kill your daughter." Winter took a tentative step forward. She was back on the edge, exactly where she'd been when that bomb went off. Her gaze drifted back to Eve, silently begging her to twitch, anything, a sign. "Eve didn't. I didn't."

Lessner seemed to weaken a little, but then he snarled and stiffened. "It's nothing personal. It just has to be done."

"That's just what Erik wants you to think. It isn't true. You can stop this. Right here, right now. You have all the power to end this nightmare and help me catch Saulson." She lowered her hands, as though she were calming an overwrought child. "Just put down the gun."

"You don't understand!" His voice cracked, and he swung the barrel around.

It was pointing at Winter's chest now. She instinctively took the tiniest step back but told herself to remain calm. The gun was off Noah, and that was all that mattered in this moment.

"He has Quincy." Tears poured down Lessner's cheeks.

"What do you mean he *has* her?"

"Everything. He has her toys and her clothes and her pictures. I can't lose her. Not again."

Winter stood frozen, her gaze darting from Noah to Eve to the gun. She didn't want to antagonize Lessner, especially with his eyes looking so manic. Was he losing his grip on reality? Erik Saulson had gotten so deep in his head that he'd convinced him his daughter's things meant that much. The man had a real knack for picking just the right people to manipulate.

None of that mattered now.

Winter balled her hands into fists. "Her stuff...it's important, and I'll help you get it back."

Lessner's upper lip pulled back like a territorial wolf. "Shut up. You can't."

"I'm so sorry. It's awful what happened to her. And we can't bring her back, you're right. But I can help you find her things. I'm starting to understand Erik and how his evil mind works."

The pistol shook in his hand. He wiped his nose on his sleeve and gritted his teeth. "I won't let that son of a bitch have her!"

"Erik doesn't want your daughter. He doesn't even want you. He wants me. He wants to hurt me, and you're helping him." Winter trembled, her lungs tight. "And I don't know why."

Lessner's shoulders slumped, and the gun shuddered in his meaty hands. "I don't either."

"Please have mercy. Don't kill me, and please don't take my husband from me. Please." She nodded to Noah, lying so peacefully, unaware of the storm raging over him. "Noah would never do anything to hurt your little girl. And neither would I."

Lessner's gaze softened still further. The very tip of the gun drooped.

"The only person I want to hurt is Erik." Winter took another step closer. "Help me. Please. Help me do that."

For a moment, he looked lost and confused. She could tell his mind—highly trained—was racing through all the rational and irrational possibilities of what could happen in the next seconds.

"He will use you up like he does everybody, and then he'll kill you too. How many innocent people will you take with you?"

Lessner shook his head hard and tightened his grip. "Erik helped me. He found out the truth about what happened to Quincy. I have to hold up my end of the bargain."

"Can you even hear yourself? You're supposed to be a cop!"

"I don't care about that anymore! My whole life has been a pointless lie since losing her." His voice cracked. "And I can see now that the system is broken, and my job…your job… it's all pointless."

"That's not true."

"What did the system ever do for my Quincy, huh? Nothing! She was murdered, and they let her killers go free." A fresh wave of tears flowed down his face. "I've been dead inside ever since. But Erik showed me I still have power."

Winter took another tentative step closer. With his breathing heavy, his eyes blurred with tears, and his arm shaky, he hadn't noticed her creeping closer. "Put the gun down, Harlan. You don't want to do this."

Lessner looked dead at her. The flash of humanity from earlier had fled, leaving nothing but the empty, lifeless eyes of a killer. "It's too late for that."

The muscles in his arm twitched as he tightened the trigger.

37

A knock at the door snapped Lessner's attention away. The handle turned, and a nurse stepped in, her face going pale as her eyes locked on the gun.

She gasped, freezing in place.

Winter didn't.

With a sharp cry, she lunged for the gun, grabbing the weapon with both hands. Turning the barrel away from her, she slammed Lessner's arm hard against the bed rail. He groaned in pain and fumbled it. The gun fell onto Noah's lap.

The nurse had vanished.

Roaring in frustration, Lessner snatched Winter's wrist and yanked her closer, catching her off guard with his strength. He threw her hard against the wall, sending her crashing into equipment. Sensors started blaring like crazy. Noah moaned and stirred.

Winter twisted, trying to get leverage as Lessner's grip crushed her arm. She freed one hand just long enough to reach for her gun and managed to yank it from the holster.

Before she could aim, Lessner lunged, slamming into her with his full weight. The impact jarred the weapon from her grip, and it hit the floor with a metallic clang. Momentum carried it skidding across the tiles, disappearing beneath Noah's bed.

Lessner snarled, tightening his hold as Winter fought to get her legs around his for leverage. They tumbled to the floor, falling over Eve's legs.

Winter's head struck the side of the bed on the way down, her vision blurring.

Lessner fell on top of her. He snatched a fistful of her hair and yanked her face up, punching it with all his might. Winter's neck snapped back, blood spraying from her lips and into her eyes. Before she could blink, he wrapped his hands around her throat and squeezed.

Winter kicked and flailed, fumbling around for her weapon. It was much too far away.

Movement caught her eye, but she couldn't turn her head. Her eyes were failing, her brain fogging from lack of air as her limbs grew weak.

"Hey, asshole!"

Lessner turned toward the voice, and something smashed him in the face, knocking his hands free. He tumbled to the side, knocking a machine on top of him.

Choking, Winter scrambled to her knees. Eve lay on the floor, propped up on one elbow with blood running down the side of her face and staining her pale hair pink. Winter did a double take. A big steel water bottle lay on the ground near Lessner. He struggled to get his bearings, tossing the heart monitor and cords off him.

Winter loped to the bed and fell over Noah. She groped the covers.

Lessner roared as he began to rise, blood dripping from under one eye. He barely gained his feet before he lowered his head, looking like a charging bull.

Her fingers wrapped around his gun. She brought it up

and leveled it at his chest. "Stop where you are! Get down on your knees!"

"Fuck you." He stomped closer, hands raised to rip her apart.

Every one of her muscles flexed. "I will shoot you in the head!"

"Do it, bitch. Do it. I don't care anymore!"

Out in the hall, there was shouting and boots racing for the room. One voice called out above the rest, "Get the staff back! Secure the area!"

Darnell.

Lessner's head tipped back. He turned to Winter with a wild smile. "I can still kill you. Then at least Erik will be fucked!" He leaped.

A gun fired, shooting a hole through Lessner's arm, tossing him off balance.

Winter startled back and glanced at Eve—still on the ground in a puddle of her own blood, but with her arm straight and her gun smoking in her hand. Their eyes met just as the door to the room burst open and cops flooded the room.

Darnell rushed at Lessner and tackled him to the ground, shouting orders all the while.

Winter lowered her gun back onto Noah's bed. She felt outside her body—floating over the scene but not really a part of it. A glance at Noah confirmed he'd slept through the whole ordeal. She scanned him head to toe, the commotion around them just a blur of activity on the edge of her periphery.

Blood oozed from the top of his hand where his IV had ripped out when she and Lessner fell into the machines, but he was otherwise unharmed.

Winter stumbled across the room, falling to her knees next to Eve and wrapping her arm around her shoulders. Eve half whispered, half mumbled something unintelligible. Winter couldn't understand her over the roar of the police subduing Lessner, handcuffing him, and yanking him out of the room.

Darnell stood, rolling his shoulders back as he fixed the cuff of his sleeve, which had come unfolded in the tussle. He scanned the room with serious brown eyes and stepped to where they crouched together on the floor. "Well done, you two. You okay?"

His words were all it took to make the brittle drywood in Winter's brain snap. "Does she look okay?"

"She looks like shit, but I was talking to you. Your face—"

"Darnell, her head is bleeding! Get her a doctor right now."

Darnell backed up to the door. "We need a doctor!"

Eve gave a heavy sigh and let her head fall against Winter's shoulder. "Fried chicken."

"Shh, don't talk. Your head is bleeding. No talking."

"Okay, babe." Eve mumbled a bit more—something about her father—and slowly fell unconscious in Winter's arms.

38

Back home at last, Noah settled onto their couch and looped his arm over Winter. His ribs still hurt, but it hurt less having her near. Though his left arm was in a sling, the doctor had said everything ought to heal on its own. Except his finger, of course.

He wiggled his hand, wondering vaguely if he could still feel it. Hard to tell with the whole hand bandaged up.

"I'm not hurting you, am I?" Winter was careful to not put any of her weight on him.

He drew her closer. "No, darlin'. The opposite."

Pots and pans banged in the kitchen. When they'd arrived home a few hours ago, he'd been delighted to find his mother sitting on the stoop waiting for him. She almost knocked him over, she'd hugged him so hard.

Winter had finally called her after rescuing Noah, and she'd booked the first flight out. Now she was doing what she did best—cooking up a storm, like she thought soaking the trauma and bad feelings in butter and bacon grease would make everything better.

It couldn't hurt. After all the hell he'd suffered over the

last few days, he was finally home. And with his two favorite women.

Well, three.

Eve sat on the couch across from them, her head still wrapped in gauze from where Detective Lessner had beaten her skull against the hospital floor. Noah didn't know the whole story yet of everything she and Winter had been through together—fighting to get to him, to save his life. Winter hadn't said much about it, other than she never could've done it without his former partner.

"*She made me eat soup,*" Winter had said. Though he wasn't entirely sure what that meant, he knew it was a good thing.

"I talked to Davenport this morning." Eve gave a great yawn and stretched her arms over the back of her chair. She was always spreading out like that—arms wide, one foot crossed on top of her other knee, making herself look big. "Forensics found traces of Noah's DNA on the hood of Lessner's personal vehicle."

His mother came into the room with a tray of glasses filled with lemonade and a pile of chips and guacamole, which she set out on the table. Noah smiled and thanked her. She gave him a kiss on the forehead.

Noah snatched up a glass and took a deep drink. Fresh squeezed and slightly creamy, blended together with some peels and sweetened condensed milk like she used to do. It tasted like childhood.

Smiling, he squeezed his wife tighter. He still felt highly strung out after what he'd been through, but every little comfort brought with it a breath that expanded his lungs and slowed his heart.

"Lunch will be ready in two shakes." His mother carried on petting his head, even as her gaze moved to Eve. "Will you be joining us, dear?"

"Thank you, Mrs. Dalton. It smells amazing. But I need to be getting home soon. My husband needs some attention."

Winter chuckled and shook her head. "Husbands. So needy."

"I know, right?" Eve shot Winter a wink. "They can be kinda cute, though."

Winter nuzzled her cheek against Noah's chest. He let out another cleansing sigh, melting into her and feeling so at home.

A knock came at the door, making all of them flinch. Winter rose to answer it as Noah and Eve watched her like a pair of guard dogs.

When she drew the door open, Noah couldn't see who was on the other side, but he recognized the voice—Ariel. Winter shot an all-clear look over her shoulder before stepping out onto the porch to talk to her.

As soon as the door clicked shut, Noah immediately missed her. It was strange, seeing as he was the one who'd been kidnapped this time, but all the while he'd been lying on that makeshift bed—broken and bleeding—all he could think about was Winter. Not whether she was coming to get him, but whether she was safe.

"I want to thank you." His gaze moved to Eve. "For not giving up on me. And for looking after Winter while I was gone. Something about soup? I don't know."

Eve wrinkled the skin around her eyes playfully. "You're a real pain in my ass, you know that?"

"Oh, yeah?"

"Even when you take sabbatical and leave the office and all logic says I don't have to worry about you and your insane issues anymore, you go and get yourself kidnapped and drag me in deeper than ever before." She stuck her tongue out at him. "You're like a zit that won't let up. Every time I pop you, you just get worse."

Noah placed his hand on his heart. "Gee, I feel so loved."

She scoffed. "Also, I don't know why you ever thought it was a good idea to be working at the damn Bureau in the first place when your wife so clearly needs you with her."

He snorted at that. That was rich, after all the crap she'd given him about his mind not being on the job because he was constantly worried about Winter. "Well, *you've* changed your tune."

"You never sang the song right in the first place." She harrumphed and crossed her arms. "Now hurry up and get better so you can look after Winter. That's your job, okay? It's your only job. And don't get kidnapped anymore. Jeez."

"Eve?"

"What?"

"Thank you."

She smiled, slapping her hands on the cushions of the couch as she stood. "Time for me to mosey on down the road, I think. Jack's really irritated. He says I'm only allowed to have one husband."

"I don't know what that means."

"That's okay." She smiled, her tiny features all squinched up tight. "I'm glad you're okay."

"Thanks."

Eve gave him a lazy salute and headed out the door. She was limping a little, her ankle twisted in the scuffle, and the bandage on her head looked like a mummy's wrap. Lessner hadn't cracked her skull, but he left a gash in the back of her head five inches long. She'd needed a lot of stitches.

When Eve pulled open the door, Noah heard Ariel's and Winter's voices. Cool wind rushed over him, carrying the fresh smell of garden flowers. He couldn't believe his plants were all still alive. It must've rained while he was gone.

39

Winter had not expected to see Ariel on her doorstep. After things at the office got a little too hot one day, and Ariel ended up held at gunpoint, Winter hadn't known if she'd ever see her assistant again.

After all, it didn't seem like working at Black Investigations was going to get less dangerous anytime soon.

Ariel's eyes widened as she took in Winter's appearance, and Winter could only imagine how nasty the bruise on her face looked where Lessner had punched her. Or the ligature marks on her neck where he'd choked her. She'd avoided examining either injury too closely in the mirror.

But her assistant looked rested, as bright-eyed and bushy-tailed as ever, with a new, tiny leather backpack slung over her shoulder. She sported a new hairstyle and dye job too—her wild, shoulder-length brown curls replaced by a fire-orange pixie cut. That was the first clue that she'd been going through some emotional stuff lately.

She hadn't said anything substantive yet, just asked about Noah and how things were going.

"I like your hair."

Ariel smiled shyly, and her hand went to the back of her neck. "Really? It's not too much?"

"Too much for what?"

"To…work for you?"

Winter was pleasantly befuddled, her head cocking like a bird assessing their own nest. "You want to come back to work?"

Ariel nodded. "I've thought about it a lot. What happened with Drug Dealer Makeup Queen Jessica Huberth and her lovesick lackey Kyle Fobb was terrifying, but I don't think I can go back to a normal job after this. So long as we can still keep all the doors locked—"

"Oh, perpetually."

"Well, then I want to come back. Is that okay?"

A laugh scratched at Winter's throat. "Yes, it's okay. As long as you understand the risks. And you know better than to share anything about me with strangers."

"I do, and I do." Ariel's expression darkened, and she looked down at her feet. "I'm so sorry about all that, Winter. I feel so stupid for believing a word he said."

"Don't feel stupid."

Winter opened her mouth to give Ariel the same line she'd been feeding her since the onset of her employment, but it stuck in her throat.

"Look, I want you to be absolutely sure about this. The fact of the matter is, even after we catch Erik Saulson, I can never guarantee you'll be safe working for me. As long as Justin Black is my brother, there're going to be obsessive fanboys like Saulson and Gardner and who knows how many others who want to mess with me, or even kill me, just to prove something."

The young woman nodded quickly, her silver moon earrings tinkling in the morning sun. "I understand."

"Do you? Because I need you to really be sure." Winter

took a deep breath. "My brother's a serial killer. I know you probably know all about the things he did, because you're a damn good researcher. But I don't know if you understand just how many people are still obsessed with him. People who watched his broadcasts on the internet and sent him money while he was on the run. Who want to be like him and want me dead."

"I know."

"Any sick thing Justin ever did might happen to me or you or anyone who gets close to me." She'd never said the words out loud before. They hurt even more than she'd expected they would.

"I'm ready this time. I won't be the weak link that breaks. I took shooting lessons. I'll keep taking them. I'm not going to flunk out of Black Investigations like I did the police academy." Ariel squared her shoulders. "I'm ready."

The absurdity of it hit Winter by surprise. She laughed and groaned all at once. "Okay, Ariel. You're on. When are you ready to start? It might be a few days 'til I get back to the office. And Noah might want me to work from home."

"When you're ready, I'm ready." She seemed like she was about to turn and go, when she stopped herself and opened up her backpack. "I almost forgot."

Ariel took out a small white envelope and held it out with two fingers.

Winter withdrew a step. "What is that?"

"I went by the office to see if you were there before coming here. I ran into a delivery guy who asked me if I could bring this to you."

A knot twisted up Winter's insides. She clutched her stomach. "Dark-haired guy? About yea tall, beard?" She held up a hand to indicate six feet.

Ariel furrowed her brow suspiciously. "Uh, yeah, now that you mention it."

"Did he say anything else?"

"No. Why? Who is he?"

The front door creaked open, and Eve stepped out, popping on her sunglasses as she breezed past them. "I've gotta head out. But we need to set something up soon, okay? Jackie is dying to meet you. He wants to cook us all dinner."

"Eve, hold on."

She stopped mid-stride and turned like a jerky windup toy. "What's up?"

"This might be from Saulson." Winter glared at the envelope, which Ariel still had pinched in her fingers. "He just dropped it off at my office."

Eve took her sunglasses off. "What's in it?"

"I'm not sure I want to know."

"Do you want me to open it?" Ariel offered.

Eve narrowed her eyes suspiciously. "Have we met?"

"Oh, sorry. Eve, this is Ariel, my assistant." Winter pressed her hand to her roiling stomach. "Ariel, this is my Eve. I mean, Special Agent Eve Taggart, FBI."

Eve smiled smugly and lifted her brows. "Well, somebody better open it. I'm dying over here."

"It feels like a necklace or something."

Eve reached into her bag and yanked out some gloves. "Here." She snapped them on and snatched the envelope from Ariel, turning it up and down. Something heavy slid back and forth.

After taking pictures, she tore open one end as Winter clenched her eyes shut, memories of Noah's severed finger churning her stomach and leaving her hands cold and clammy. She reminded herself that Noah was right inside, safe and sound. No blood on the envelope and no room for a severed anything.

Winter peeked as Eve reached a pen into the envelope

and lifted out a stainless steel ball chain. "I think we found Noah's dog tags."

Winter moved in closer until she could read the name etched into the little tag.

"Don't touch them." Eve held out her hand to Ariel. "I'll take them back to the lab for processing."

"What the hell?" Winter edged closer. "Why would he give back his dog tags?"

Eve's gaze landed on Winter, her eyes wide. "Start of another game?"

The words struck like a death knell, and Winter shivered. Saulson was still out there, still using all his resources to come up with new and unique ways to mess with her, and now he had Noah's social security number and blood type. It wasn't going to stop. His games would keep going, on and on. Forever.

Ariel pressed both hands to her mouth, her eyes wide and round. "What's going on? Am I missing something?"

"A lot." Eve put her sunglasses back on. "You know what I think? I think he wants to get caught. So he's not going to stop until he's in handcuffs, and maybe not even then."

"Maybe not even then…?"

Eve bit her lip. "Who knows how many pins he has set up ready to fall?"

Winter nodded gravely, the truth settling over her like a wet blanket. She'd saved Noah, and they'd caught Lessner, but that was just one battle in Erik Saulson's massive, drawn-out assault. He'd given her everything she'd needed to win. Every clue, every opportunity. It was like he was building her up for something, but what?

The big boss battle, of course.

Winter turned away from the other two women and gazed out over her garden—at Noah's clematis.

Saulson had done everything he could think of to try and

break her—stealing and mutilating her husband, isolating her, tormenting her with damn puzzles. But she'd come through it. Winter wasn't made of glass.

"It doesn't matter," she said at last, turning back to Eve and Ariel. "No matter what he throws at us, he won't win. He doesn't realize it yet, but he's outgunned, outsmarted, and outnumbered." She sucked in a long, determined breath. "He's fighting a losing war, and we're going to crush him."

40

That night, after a heavy dinner and a long bath, Winter climbed into bed beside her husband and cuddled up under his right arm. She couldn't remember the last time she'd felt so tired, yet she didn't want to fall asleep. She didn't even want to blink…she was so scared Noah might disappear.

Pressing her face into his chest, she drank in his musky, sugary scent and brushed her cheek against his skin. Emotions crashed over her, the fear and the pain of the last few days coming in waves, but they receded just as quickly as they rose. The storm was over. Now she just had to put herself back together.

Except it wasn't over. It hadn't ended when they'd caught Carl Gardner or Cybil Kerie. And it wouldn't end now simply because they had Detective Harlan Lessner in custody. As long as Erik Saulson was free, he would never stop.

The killer had led her through a twisted game of cat and mouse. But this wasn't just any maze. It was Winter's maze, and she intended to win.

"He's still out there." Winter propped herself up on an

elbow to look into Noah's forest-green eyes. "We didn't get any closer to finding him. I have nothing. We don't even have his real name because we still can't find him."

Noah combed the fingers of his right hand through her wet hair. "Baby, give yourself a break. You found me. You saved me. You're amazing."

She gently rested her head back on his chest and wrapped her leg over his. He looped his bandaged hand under her knee and gently pulled her closer.

"I can't let up now. Taking any time off will just be giving him space to lay his next horrible trap. I'll work from home the next few days so I can look after you. I have an office here. I never use it, but I have one."

Noah shook his head. "My mom's got that covered. You've spent enough time driving yourself crazy over me. I'm good."

"You're the most important person in my entire world, and I wouldn't know how to live without you." Winter squeezed him tighter than she probably should have, her eyelids clenching shut as a silent tear squeezed out.

He kissed her forehead. "It's okay, baby. I'm here. I'm safe. You saved me."

Her throat tightened. "I have to stop him."

"You will. And that's why you're going into work tomorrow with a clear head that isn't worried about me. And you're going to figure this out. Because you're Winter Black, and no moron criminal could ever outsmart you."

She tilted her head up. His smile and his open, honest eyes were stronger than three shots of espresso and sweeter than any of Grandma Beth's perfect brownies. "I love you. I'm gonna get that son of a bitch that hurt you."

"I know you will."

The need to kiss him overwhelmed every other thought in Winter's head. She needed to be closer to him—to feel him on every inch of her skin. She pressed her hands to either side of his face, drinking him in. Then she moved her kisses over his chin, his cheek, his neck.

Noah moaned and moved his hand under her shirt to lay his palm on the flat of her back.

Winter broke off the kiss and looked into his eyes, her hips pulling tighter to his. "Can we? I'll be so gentle."

"Yes, please."

With a giggle that felt like warm spring rain on her tired, dehydrated heart, she kissed him and drew herself up to straddle his hips. Winter had grabbed the edges of her loose silk pajama shirt to draw it off over her head when her phone rang where it lay charging on her nightstand.

She glanced at the screen and bit her lip.

"Who is it? Don't answer."

"It's Eve." Still sitting on her husband's lap, Winter snatched up her phone and put it on speaker. "Hey. What's up?"

Before Eve even spoke, Winter knew something was wrong. Her voice scratched like wind on rocks. "Do you want the good news or the bad news?"

Noah pushed himself up on his elbows, staring intently. "What's the bad news?"

"Lessner escaped."

All the blood drained from Winter's face. "What? How?"

"I don't know the details, but he was in transit and faked a heart attack. He killed an officer. He's out there, still trying to follow Saulson's orders."

Winter had to start her next sentence twice before it took. "What's the good news?"

"The good news is those tags he sent to you had a print on them, and I just got a match. I know Erik Saulson's real name."

The End
To be continued...

Thank you for reading.
All of the Winter Black Series books can be found on Amazon.

ACKNOWLEDGMENTS

The past few years have been a whirlwind of change, both personally and professionally, and I find myself at a loss for the right words to express my profound gratitude to those who have supported me on this remarkable journey. Yet, I am compelled to try.

To my sons, whose unwavering support has been my bedrock, granting me the time and energy to transform my darkest thoughts into words on paper. Your steadfast belief in me has never faltered, and watching each of you grow, welcoming the wonderful daughters you've brought into our family, has been a source of immense pride and joy.

Embarking on the dual role of both author and publisher has been an exhilarating, albeit challenging, adventure. Transitioning from the solitude of writing to the dynamic world of publishing has opened new horizons for me, and I'm deeply grateful for the opportunity to share my work directly with you, the readers.

I extend my heartfelt thanks to the entire team at Mary Stone Publishing, the same dedicated group who first recognized my potential as an indie author years ago. Your collective efforts, from the editors whose skillful hands have polished my words to the designers, marketers, and support staff who breathe life into these books, have been instrumental in resonating deeply with our readers. Each of you plays a crucial role in this journey, not only nurturing my growth but also ensuring that every story reaches its full potential. Your dedication, creativity, and finesse have been nothing short of invaluable.

However, my deepest gratitude is reserved for you, my beloved readers. You ventured off the beaten path of traditional publishing to embrace my work, investing your most precious asset—your time. It is my sincerest hope that this book has enriched that time, leaving you with memories that linger long after the last page is turned.

With all my love and heartfelt appreciation,

Mary

ABOUT THE AUTHOR

Nestled in the serene Blue Ridge Mountains of East Tennessee, Mary Stone crafts her stories surrounded by the natural beauty that inspires her. What was once a home filled with the lively energy of her sons has now become a peaceful writer's retreat, shared with cherished pets and the vivid characters of her imagination.

As her sons grew and welcomed wonderful daughters-in-law into the family, Mary's life entered a quieter phase, rich with opportunities for deep creative focus. In this tranquil environment, she weaves tales of courage, resilience, and intrigue, each story a testament to her evolving journey as a writer.

From childhood fears of shadowy figures under the bed to a profound understanding of humanity's real-life villains, Mary's style has been shaped by the realization that the most complex antagonists often hide in plain sight. Her writing is characterized by strong, multifaceted heroines who defy traditional roles, standing as equals among their peers in a world of suspense and danger.

Mary's career has blossomed from being a solitary author to establishing her own publishing house—a significant milestone that marks her growth in the literary world. This expansion is not just a personal achievement but a reflection of her commitment to bring thrilling and thought-provoking stories to a wider audience. As an author and publisher, Mary continues to challenge the conventions of the thriller genre, inviting readers into gripping tales filled with serial killers, astute FBI agents, and intrepid heroines who confront peril with unflinching bravery.

Each new story from Mary's pen—or her publishing house—is a pledge to captivate, thrill, and inspire, continuing the legacy of the imaginative little girl who once found wonder and mystery in the shadows.

Discover more about Mary Stone on her website.
www.authormarystone.com

- facebook.com/authormarystone
- x.com/MaryStoneAuthor
- goodreads.com/AuthorMaryStone
- bookbub.com/authors/mary-stone
- pinterest.com/MaryStoneAuthor
- instagram.com/marystoneauthor

Printed in Great Britain
by Amazon